ON THE THRESHHOLD OF THE TOWERS OF HIGH SORCERY

During the night, a mist-shroudeded forest magically appeared before your campsite. You recognized it instantly as the mysterious Wayreth Forest, the last barrier that stands between you and your destination—the fabled Towers of High Sorcery.

But now, as you and your brother Caramon make your way along the foggy forest path, the mists ahead of you suddenly part. Facing you is a hooded, glowing spectral figure, who raises one hand, points it straight at you, and begins to advance toward you!

You realize you've only a few moments to cast a spell at the mysterious spectral being.

What spell will you cast?

Turn to section **10** and locate the spell you wish to cast along one side of the Spell Resolution Table. Then cross-index the spell you have chosen with the number of the section you are reading. Turn to the numbered section that you will find where the two columns meet to find out the results of your spell.

Whatever the outcome, only your decisions, and the luck of the dice roll, can help you pass the Test of **THE SOULFORGE**

An ADVANCED DUNGEONS & DRAGONS™
Adventure Gamebook #4

The SOULFORGE

BY TERRY PHILLIPS

Cover Art by Keith Parkinson
Interior Art by Mark Nelson

TSR, Inc.
PRODUCTS OF YOUR IMAGINATION™

To Raistlin,
who is more alive
than he'll ever know . . .

Distributed to the book trade in the United States by Random House, Inc., and in Canada by Random House of Canada, Ltd.

Distributed in the United Kingdom by TSR UK, Ltd. Distributed to the toy and hobby trade by regional distributors.

ADVANCED DUNGEONS & DRAGONS and AD&D are registered trademarks owned by TSR, Inc.

DRAGONLANCE, SUPER ENDLESS QUEST, PICK A PATH TO ADVENTURE, PRODUCTS OF YOUR IMAGINATION, and the TSR logo are trademarks owned by TSR, Inc.

First printing: September, 1985
Printed in the United States of America
Library of Congress Catalog Card Number: 85-90158
ISBN: 0-88038-254-6

9 8 7 6 5 4 3 2 1

TSR, Inc.
P.O. Box 756
Lake Geneva, WI 53147

TSR UK, Ltd.
The Mill, Rathmore Road
Cambridge CB1 4AD
United Kingdom

AN EXCITING NEW EXPERIENCE IN BOOKS!

Welcome, you who are about to endure the Test of THE SOULFORGE, to an exciting, totally new concept in role-playing gamebooks.

Based on the popular ADVANCED DUNGEONS & DRAGONS® Game, Adventure Gamebooks require only two standard six-sided dice, an ample supply of luck—and, most of all, your skill in making decisions as you play the game. If dice are unavailable, a simple alternative, requiring only pencil and paper, may be used instead.

ADVANCED DUNGEONS & DRAGONS® Adventure Gamebooks read easily, without complicated rules to slow down the story. Once you have read through the simple rules that follow, you should seldom find it necessary to refer back to them. Your options are repeated clearly in the text at each choice point, with occasional reminders about additional options you may wish to consider to improve your chances. Your adventure reads like a book, plays like a game, and offers a thrill a minute—with YOU as the hero!

YOUR CHARACTER

In this book, you are Raistlin of Solace, a moody, hot-tempered, brilliant young magic-user from the village of Solace. Your world is the world of Krynn, from THE DRAGONLANCE™ CHRONICLES, peopled by all manner of strange beings and creatures.

For as long as you remember, you have been able to read and detect magic inherently, a fact noted with a great deal of attention by the citizens of Solace. Some expect great things of you; others warn that you will bring damnation upon their village.

But all that must occupy the back of your mind for now, as you set out upon your greatest challenge—to journey to the fabled Towers of High Sorcery, there to face the dreaded Test that all great mages must pass!

PLAYING THE GAME

ESTABLISHING YOUR CHARACTER

YOUR Raistlin of Solace will be different from someone else's because YOU help to create him.

Carefully tear out the removable **Character Stats Card** at the beginning of this book. This card is your record of Raistlin's character makeup. It also doubles as a bookmark.

Since you will probably be playing this adventure many times, we suggest that you write on the card lightly and in pencil only, so that your character stats can be erased easily when you are ready to play again. If you have access to a photocopier, you may wish to make photocopies of the Character Stats Card before you fill it in. Another alternative is to reproduce the card on a 3"x 5" card or a slip of paper.

You are now ready to complete the individual identity of Raistlin by establishing his strengths and weaknesses. Your character's **name** (Raistlin) and **character class** (Magic-user) have already been entered for you. Before you fill out the rest of the card, it is necessary for you to understand the game's scoring system.

SCORING

Playing the game requires you to keep track of three things—**hit points, skill points**, and **experience points**—on the tear-out **Character Stats Card** located at the front of the book. An explanation of each of these follows.

HIT POINTS

As Raistlin, you have a specific life strength, represented by **hit points**. Once your character's hit points are gone, he ceases to exist, and the adventure has ended, whether the text has come to an end or not.

Raistlin may lose hit points when he fails, through the roll of the dice, to subdue an enemy with a magic spell or outwit the enemy, because the opponent strikes him back. As a result, you must deduct a stated number of hit points from Raistlin's hit point total.

A character may also lose hit points through sneak attacks or through carelessness when he has no chance to fight back. In such instances, roll the stated number of dice for **damage**. The result of the die roll is deducted from the character's total hit points and recorded on the Character Stats Card.

Raistlin, as a young magic-user, a class not known for strength, starts out with 6 hit points, plus two random chances to improve this score. Roll one six-sided die twice and add the the higher number of the two scores to 6 for your total hit points. Record this number in the blank space labeled "hit points."

Guard Raistlin's hit points carefully, but don't be too cautious about losing them when the goal seems worthwhile. At times throughout the adventure, you may have the opportunity to recover some of your hit points through healing or rest. However, it's important to remember that *you can never recover more hit points than you had at the start of your adventure.*

SKILL POINTS

Now you are ready to determine the **skills** of your characters.

Skill points allow you to increase a character's chances of success by adding the score for a specific skill to the dice roll. In this book, you will be asked to divide 9 skill points in any way you want for Raistlin, with one exception. As a magic-user, Raistlin's reasoning skill score must be the highest, or equal to the highest, of the three skill scores, and his presence skill score must be the lowest, or equal to the lowest. All three skills *must* have at least one skill point assigned. An explanation of each of your three skills—**reasoning**, **agility**, and **presence** follows.

Reasoning

A magic-user's **reasoning** power is his most important skill. It enables him to think through all aspects of a situation quickly, frequently while under great pressure.

When you use your reasoning skill in this book, roll one die and add the result to your reasoning skill score. If the total is equal to, or larger than, the number required (given in the text), you are successful.

Agility

Raistlin's **agility** skill score increases his chances of success in feats involving such things as nimbleness, dexterity, speed, dodging, and the like.

To use your agility skill, roll one die and add the result to your agility skill score. If the total is equal to, or greater than, the number given in the text, you have succeeded.

Presence

Your **presence** skill score increases your chances of success in keeping cool under pressure without panicking. It also helps you to convince others to act as you wish them to. Thus its use can frequently influence the decisions of others.

To use your presence skill, roll one die and add the result to your presence skill score. If the total equals or exceeds the number given in the text, you are successful.

EXPERIENCE POINTS

As in real life, experience increases chances of success in a given situation because you have encountered a similar situation before and understand the possibilities that may occur. You, as Raistlin, begin this adventure with precisely 6 **experience points**. You may spend them to increase your chances on *any* die roll throughout the book, but once experience points are used up, they are gone and must be deducted from your total. We suggest you save as many as you can in this adventure, for at some point, you may be judged by them.

To use experience points, you must decide how many points you will spend *before* you roll the die, then add that score to the die roll. Whether the roll of the die is successful or not, the experience points are gone and must be deducted from your total.

Use your experience points wisely, saving them for crucial situations. At a number of places in this story, you may be rewarded with extra experience points for playing the adventure well.

MAGIC USE

A magic-user must memorize the spells he plans to use for any given adventure. Certain spells also require use of a spell component—perhaps a bit of bat fur, a lizard's tail, and so forth.

At the start of this adventure, you may assume that Raistlin is prepared to use any spell in his spellbook (section **10**) and that he has brought along the proper components for any spells listed. He must, of course, have the components in hand and ready to use. At some point in the story, he may lose his spell components. If so, he must somehow acquire the proper components for each spell he wishes to cast in order to use it. If at any time, you, as Raistlin, try to cast a spell that requires a component and you do not have it with you, you *must* turn to section **193**.

Likewise, spells must be reviewed periodically in order to use them properly. At the adventure's beginning, Raistlin has reviewed all his spells and thus may use any of them. But as time goes on, he may forget their proper wording and must review them again. The text will explain how to know which spells are available to Raistlin at any given time.

PLAYING WITHOUT DICE

Should you ever wish to play the adventure when dice are unavailable, there is a simple substitute that requires only pencil and paper. Simply write the numbers 1 through 6 on separate slips of paper and mix them up in a container. Then draw one of the slips, note the number, and place it back in the container. Mix up the numbers and draw a second time. Each draw represents one roll of a die. If only one die is called for, draw only one number.

Your character is now complete, and you are ready to begin your adventure. Turn the page—and good luck!

"Why must we test this one so severely?" whispered a voice from the nether region.

"Who questions the gods?" Par-Salian muttered impatiently. "They demanded a sword; I found one. But beaten . . . tempered . . . made useful."

"And if he breaks?" hissed the shadow voice.

"Then we bury the pieces!"

From the Chronicles of
Astinus of Palanthus of
Krynn

1

The spot of light shimmering on the floor of the vast mountain valley looks small and inconsequential from such a height. It is particularly extraordinary that it should be here in the middle of her territory, which covers much of the western reaches of the Kharolis Mountains. But as the night-hunting owl drops on silent wings to investigate, the light grows and grows, until it becomes something rarely seen in this part of the world of Krynn—a campfire.

As the owl floats downward in the moonless darkness, her night senses gather in more of the singular scene—the sound of horses shuffling about restlessly, a small lean-to, and two human creatures gathered around the light. One of them is a large, burly thing, well muscled and strong. She does not know that this is a warrior—and a very strong one at that. She has never really seen one before. This type of creature has never been here before, as far as she can remember.

The other, her senses recognize immediately. Smaller, thinner, not as strong. She has sensed many of this type in her valley at previous times, though the word *magician* means nothing to her.

But from this smaller figure there emanates an indefinable power that unnerves her, a power stronger than any she has ever felt before. Her instincts read it as clearly as one reads a scroll in broad daylight.

Disquieted, she digs her wings into the still night air and sweeps off across the valley to continue her night hunt in the wooded peaks beyond. Turn to **94**.

2

The early afternoon sun beats down on you as you journey up the winding road to Verdin. Once you are past the foothills, the road climbs steeply up the face of the slope to the city. You are hot and tired from the long climb.

As you near the city's walls, you welcome their cool shade. The town seems smaller than you first thought. You note that the walls and gate seem to be crumbling, the fields are barren, and the livestock ridden with disease.

The guards at the city's gate are dressed in the poorest excuse for livery you have ever seen. What few children you see running about are dirty and hungry-looking. You conclude that this place has been wanting for even the bare necessities for some time.

Once at the gate, you can hear the sounds of some sort of a festival from inside the city. The walls of the castle and other buildings are draped with all manner of bright decorations. Music rings from the parapets and floats out over the walls of the town. The festive mood has even affected the guards at the gate, who allow you to approach without so much as a "State your name and business." In fact, joviality has loosened the guards' tongues, helped along by large quantities of wine they are consuming.

"A toasht to our new cleric!" slurs the captain of the guard, lurching to his one side and raising his wine flagon. Flagons are quickly taken up by his companions.

"And a great man he ish, too," the captain continues. "He brought ush hope out of ruin and deshpair with hish meshages of the new gods. Here'sh to long proshperity under hish gui—hic!—dance!"

"Tell me," you ask, instantly mindful of the many false clerics you've seen on Krynn since the Cataclysm, "does this cleric have a name?"

"Of coursh," one of the other guards blurts. "Everybody hash a name, right? Hish name ish . . . uh, Verimard . . . uh, no, it's Verdimnard . . . uh, Verminaard! Yup, thash it! Hard to shay, but that'sh no matter. He'sh here and we're—hic!—shaved! To hish health!"

As another round of drinks is poured and flagons are raised, you pass through the gate and into the city.

It's easy to see why these villagers would accept almost anyone who promised better times. The squalor of the streets and the pathetic condition of the townspeople vaguely remind you of an earlier experience in your life.

Still, signs of merriment are everywhere. Crowds of townspeople throng the streets, dancing and singing.

You fail to be caught up in the spirit of celebration, however, as your mind mulls over what the guard said about the town's new cleric and his "new gods." You remember the days when you, Caramon, Tanis Half-Elven, and your other friends would travel the countryside trying to right the wrongs of these self-proclaimed emissaries from the so-called new gods. As you make your way toward the town square, nagging doubts surface in your mind once more.

I've been to this town before, I swear it! Why do I know this place and how is it a part of my Test? Just then your thoughts are interrupted by a shout from somewhere in front of you, in the direction of the town square. "He comes! He comes!" someone cries loudly, and the crowd surges forward, carrying you along with it.

Turn to **110**.

3

You've never seen anything move so fast! You haven't even begun your spell before the drow's hand comes up holding a small crossbow. In a flash, the dart flies unerringly across the cavern, straight at your heart!

You twist to the side, trying to dodge. The dart misses your heart but pierces your shoulder, its impact slamming you up against the wall. In moments, you begin to feel numb.

The dart was drugged!

Turn to **157**.

4

You can almost feel the Sleep spell fall upon the lead dragonman. You watch tensely, hoping your spell will have the desired effect.

Slowly the leader's eyes blink. Its head bobs, then nods, and finally drops to its chest. Then its knees buckle and it

17

falls straight into the pot of gully dwarves!

The other two dragonmen are alerted by the clang of their leader's mace as it strikes the pot. They look up just in time to see their leader's legs disappear through the hole in the floor as the pot begins to descend. With a shriek, they leap across the room and dive into the hole in an attempt to save their commander.

Suddenly you feel very strange. You look up to see the walls of the chamber beginning to shimmer with a strange, iridescent light, as if some powerful magic is at work! Turn to **123**.

5

The mists part to reveal a broad clearing in the path, about fifty feet across. At its far edge stands a single figure. It appears to be a man.

The figure is heavily shrouded by his robes, which are as red as your own, and he appears to be about your height. He stands with his head slightly bowed, causing his hood to drape over his face. His hands are hidden within the voluminous folds of his sleeves.

Your senses tell you that this is no ordinary being. A dim glow curls about his robes, lightly illuminating the fog near him. But somehow you are not entirely sure that he is there at all. He seems faintly translucent. You realize as well that the cold that you have felt for the past several minutes emanates from this being.

You gather your nerve to address the stranger. You try to show respect in your tone for the obvious power flowing from this apparition.

"Hail, revered stranger," you call out. "I am called Raistlin. I have been summoned by the mage Par-Salian to seek the Test within the Towers of High Sorcery. This warrior is my brother, Caramon. We are both much honored by your presence and seek a boon of you. We would like to know if you are sent to guide us to the illustrious towers."

The hooded figure neither moves nor answers.

As you consider this, you hear Caramon's voice from behind you. "Ho, minion!" Caramon booms, finally having brought his horse under control. "If you are sent to guide us, be quick about it! If not, stand aside and we will find these towers ourselves!"

Your brother's brazen words make you wince. You whirl on him, enraged. "Caramon, you oaf!" you whisper tensely. "Will you never learn to mind your own business? This is my affair, and I will handle it!"

A hollow voice breaks in on your tirade. Dark and empty with death, it knifes through the air and the mist and fills your mind. You turn to see the hooded man moving toward you. He stops about halfway across the clearing and raises his head slightly. His face remains shrouded by the hood.

"I am sent as a guide for him who seeks the Test," he intones, "but all I find is a loud-mouthed fool, accompanied by a child in robes. Surely you do not presume to match your puny skills against the Test?" he says, turning straight toward you. "This is a jest, is it not?"

You are too stunned to reply. Then a slight movement catches the corner of your sight. You cast a quick glance at Caramon. He's drawing his sword!

Roll one die and add the result to your presence ability score. If the total is 6 or more, turn to **9**. If it is less than 6, turn to **124**.

6

The meal that was left for you is every bit as good as the last one. More gratifying still was the short note nestled alongside your dinner.

"Congratulations! You have made it back safely once again. Enjoy your meal and renew your strength with rest, for the next phase of your Test will be more trying than the previous two combined. Feel free to take whatever spell components you think you can use—but take no more than four. Choose wisely."

Having eaten your fill, you rise to examine the shelves and replenish your supply of spell components.

But you quickly realize that things are not as you remember them. To your surprise, some of the bottles have been left open. Others are knocked over and broken, their components missing. From what's left, you make up the following list:

talc	powdered silver
bitumen	powdered diamonds
umber hulk blood	soot
phosphorus	licorice root
mandrake root	snakes' tongues
liquid pitch	eyelashes in gum arabic
hen hearts	lumps of wax
bat guano/sulphur balls	

You look around the room warily. *Someone has been here while I've been gone. Is someone else using this room as well? Could it be that there's another magic-user undergoing the Test at the same time as I?*

You decide that such questions are better left to another time. Right now, you need to gather your spell components.

Once again, write the components you select on the back of your Character Stats Card. Make sure you choose only four components in all. Remember, it's very important to have the right component when casting a spell.

After you have selected some of your spell components,

roll one die and add the result to your reasoning skill score. If the total is 7 or more, turn to **91**. If it is less than 7, select the rest of your four components and turn to **78**.

7

Not only does the strange image of the bully disappear, but the entire town begins to fade away as well. The great vallenwood trees vanish into thin air, and you find yourself alone at the fork in the road. The sign pointing to Verdin stands there as before.

You stand alongside the road with a warm feeling inside. You've come this far in your Test and have managed to get by pretty well. You're almost whistling as you start out on the road to Verdin.

Add 2 experience points to your total and go to **2**.

8

You don't need to consider the great mage's offer for long. Successful completion of the Test is all that matters to you. You'd be willing to pay any price.

"Great One," you reply respectfully, "I am your humble servant. I accept your gracious offer." *Besides,* you think rapidly, *the time will come when I turn this exchange to my advantage. Then we will see what we will see!*

Fistandantalus chuckles happily. "Well said, young mage. The pact is sealed. Now for the aid I promised you. I have two gifts for you.

"First," he says with a wave of his hand, "I give you a full complement of spell components. You will find them in your robe. You are free to use any spell you have at your command during the last phase of the trial. Secondly, take this." He reaches inside his robes and pulls out a scroll.

"This scroll contains a Continual Light spell, something you will definitely need during the final phase of your Test. Use it wisely. You should know when."

As you slide the scroll into your sash, Fistandantalus watches you appraisingly. At last he speaks. "Go now. Make good use of my gifts. And remember, together we can conquer anything—even the world!"

With an arcane gesture, he vanishes and the room fades around you. Turn to **120**.

9

As you watch Caramon slide his sword from its sheath, a thought curdles your insides. *He means to defend my honor,* you think angrily.

Caramon's interference and the guide's insults are too much. Rage rises hotly within you and pushes aside all other considerations.

"Caramon, put your sword away and stand aside!" you command icily. "I will see to this matter without your help!" You brush by him brusquely and stride forward toward your taunter.

"I am he who seeks the Test," you shout. "State your business with me and be gone. We have traveled far, and have neither the time nor the inclination to deal with a lowborn messenger boy!"

The figure stiffens his back at your lashing words. "Bold you are," he replies, "but so they warned me. That much is good. But you are also arrogant! You have much to learn, young mage, particularly where respect for your betters is concerned. Very well, then. My business with you will not take long!"

You watch as he pulls a hand from his sleeve. Raising it steadily, he advances toward you, his hand glowing spectrally. You realize at last what the creature is when a wave of incredible fear suddenly overcomes you. Your body and soul are hammered by the spell's ferocious onslaught. Despite its force, you manage to remain on your feet. You see Caramon leap from his horse and draw his sword, crouching between you and the advancing robed figure.

22

You know what your brother will do if given the chance. It would be disastrous, for you now know what he is up against. You have only seconds to decide what to do before the situation becomes irreversible.

If you tell Caramon to stand aside and let the spectre approach you, turn to **156**. If you decide to let Caramon intercept the figure, turn to **49**. If you elect to cast a spell at the spectre, turn to **88**. If you think you should back away from this spectral minion, go to **22**.

10
RAISTLIN'S SPELLBOOK

The following spells are the basic ones found in Raistlin's Spellbook, and are therefore the only ones available for him to use, *unless he has been supplied with additional spells from some other source.* If he has, you will be told about them in the text. The information should be interpreted as follows:

Name of spell; OFFensive, DEFensive, or MISCellaneous in character; description of spell's effect; area or range of effect; maximum number of objects or creatures affected by the spell; material components needed to cast the spell, if any. NA means "not applicable."

FIRST LEVEL SPELLS

Burning Hands; OFF; fanlike sheet of flames shoots forth from outstretched hands; 3 feet in front of magic-user; 3 maximum; no components.
Charm Person; OFF; charmed creature believes magic-user is a trusted friend who must be heeded and protected; 120 feet; 1 maximum; no components.
Comprehend Languages; MISC, DEF; magic-user can read or understand any written or spoken language; touch; 1 object or creature; pinch of soot and a few grains of salt.
Hold Portal; DEF; magically bars or locks door, valve, or gate; 6 feet or 80 square feet; 1 door, valve, or gate; no components.
Magic Missile; OFF; causes magic darts to shoot from

magic-user's hands; 90 feet; 2 maximum; no components, needed.

Push; OFF; causes invisible force to strike any object magic-user points at; 47 feet; 1 object or creature maximum; pinch of powdered brass.

Sleep; OFF; causes slumber to fall upon one or more creatures; 60 feet or 30 foot diameter circle; 8 maximum; pinch of fine sand, rose petals, or a live cricket.

Tenser's Floating Disc; MISC; magic-user creates a gravityless circle three feet above ground; 20 feet or 3 feet in diameter; 2 maximum; a drop of mercury.

SECOND LEVEL SPELLS

Audible Glamer; DEF; magic-user causes loud noise, such as a group of people, to come from any direction chosen; 90 foot hearing range; any number; small bit of wool or lump of wax.

Darkness 15′; DEF or OFF; causes total, impenetrable darkness in affected area; 30 foot diameter; 8-12 maximum; a drop of pitch or piece of coal.

ESP (Extra-Sensory Perception); DEF; magic-user detects surface thoughts of any creature in range; 15 feet; 1 creature per attempt; a piece of copper.

Invisibility; DEF; causes recipient to vanish, not to be detected by normal vision; touch; 1 maximum; eyelash encased in a bit of gum arabic.

Mirror Image; DEF; creates 4 exact images of magic-user in range; circle 12 feet in diameter; NA; no components.

Web; OFF; creates mass of strong, sticky strands of webbing; 15 feet, or 80 cubic feet in front of magic-user (comparable to an area 40′ × 2′ × 1′); 8-12 maximum; a bit of spiderweb.

SPELL RESOLUTION TABLE

When you are ready to cast a spell, simply cross-index the line containing the spell you wish to cast with the column headed by the number of the section you are currently reading. At the juncture of these two columns, you will find a number. This number is the section number you must turn to to continue reading the story. Be sure to follow whatever instructions are contained in the entry you read. Also be sure you have the proper spell components to cast your spell if they are needed.

	100	52	119	197	160	202	20	129 115
*Audible Glamer (wool or wax)	116	121	38	39	193	53	53	83
Burning Hands	171	133	38	136	187	225	225	83
Charm Person	116	198	38	136	187	31	98	83
*Comprehend Languages (soot and salt)	116	121	38	33	209	193	193	83
*Darkness 15′ (pitch or coal)	116	121	38	39	213	183	183	83
*Detect Invisibility (talc and powdered silver)	116	121	38	33	193	225	225	83
*ESP (piece of copper)	116	121	38	39	187	193	193	83
Hold Portal	116	177	38	33	217	225	225	83
*Invisibility (eyelash in gum arabic)	116	121	38	39	44	225	225	126
Magic Missile	28	127	38	136	187	86	172	40
Mirror Image	68	177	38	39	190	225	225	184
Push (powdered brass)	116	121	38	136	193	105	71	83
*Sleep (sand, rose petals, or cricket)	90	121	38	148	187	77	111	83
*Tenser's Floating Disc (mercury)	116	121	38	33	187	193	193	83
*Web (spiderweb)	116	121	38	39	187	128	218	174

*If at any time you attempt to cast a spell marked with an asterisk without having the proper spell component(s), turn straight to **193**.

You rein in your horse directly in front of the figure blocking the great gate. Exercising immense control of both your animal and your trembling heart, you address the guardian. Your response is brash, and the anger in your voice is impossible to miss.

"I am the mage, Raistlin," you say menacingly. "I have been summoned here to be put to the Test at the command of Par-Salian, the Great One himself. But if this is the way guests to the Towers are treated, perhaps I will forget the invitation. I grow weary of this game!"

You half expect this powerful minion to destroy you on the spot. But you no longer care. You are frustrated at being challenged by this being for a second time.

The hooded figure looks in your direction briefly. Then, to your surprise, he throws back his head and roars in deep, hollow laughter.

"Well spoken, youngster. Ever the impetuous one. But I understand your impatience. I only hope it doesn't get you killed once the Test begins. Proceed!"

He stands aside and waves you in. Add 1 experience point to your total and turn to **147**.

12

The raging flame engulfs you. Your robes ignite instantly, and you become a burning pillar of fire. You hear your own flesh crackling, splitting, charring; your hair shrivels and crinkles. The searing heat scalds your lungs, and they collapse inside your chest. You slump in a charred heap to the floor.

You are conscious just long enough to see your opponent standing over you. You realize, in terrible, screaming agony, that you very nearly succeeded.

Fistandantalus's hollow voice enters your mind. "So much promise," it whispers, "but so little wisdom. So much depended upon you, Raistlin, but you wouldn't learn. Now you are of no use to anyone!" All grows silent and you do not hear the voice again.

If only I'd been a little wiser, a little faster. If only I'd . . . if only . . . if . . .

Turn to **18**.

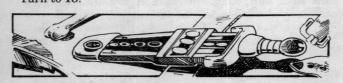

13

The gang leader can't hold your steady gaze. His eyes shift nervously back and forth to his companions, as though waiting for them to make the first move. They, in turn, seem to be waiting for a command from him. It's obvious to you that your words have taken some of the starch out of them.

Slowly the leader of the gang drops his gaze to the ground and throws his club into the undergrowth at the side of the road.

"Well, I guess that little trick you pulled on us was a pretty long time ago," he mutters, half under his breath. "I guess I'm big enough to forgive and forget, eh? What do you say, boys? Let's just let it pass, shall we?"

His cronies are quick to agree. One by one, they begin to move off into the trees. Soon the only one who is left is their leader.

As soon as his companions have gone, the gang leader straightens his back and looks up at you. You're startled to see a broad smile spread across his face. Turn to **214**.

14

Fear of death seems to take complete control of your mind, completely destroying your confidence. Finally you rein in your horse.

"No," you whisper, "we will not proceed. You are right, Caramon. The way to the towers cannot lie through this miserable forest. There must be another way. We will circle around this wood or choose other trails until we find the towers. But I feel certain we will only find our deaths here in this godforsaken forest."

Without warning, before your startled eyes, the forest begins to vanish. It seems to dissolve into the surrounding mist. Soon all that remains is a grassy valley stretching out before you. The wind whispers softly through the grass as it passes.

Suddenly a voice speaks from the air around you. You recognize it as that of the Master, Par-Salian. Turn to **210**.

15

The stone under your back is cold and hard. *Odd,* you think, *I wouldn't have thought that one could be aware of such sensations when he was dead.*

You begin to investigate other parts of your body. The damage you took should be wracking you with pain, but strangely enough, you feel little pain.

Not so strange, your mind chides you. *You're dead, remember? Dead men don't feel anything!*

Well, then, why does my back hurt? the more reasonable side of your brain queries. *And where is that light coming from?* You turn your head to the left and see a shaft of light beaming down from an unknown height. It forms a circle of light at the far end of the great hall you find yourself lying in. In the center of that circle is a throne, and on the throne, heavily shrouded in black robes, sits a man! As you rise to your feet, he speaks to you.

"Welcome back," he says in a dusty, sand-filled voice that seems to echo hollowly down a long tunnel.

"B-Back?" you stammer. "You mean I was—"

"Yes, yes," he interrupts, somewhat impatiently, "you were dead. But you are too valuable to lose just now, so I decided to bend the rules a little and keep you with us. It seemed a pity that you had come so far, only to be stopped by an unfortunate miscalculation on your part."

"But—but how can that be?" you ask. "I thought the Test required—"

"Do not concern yourself with the Test," the figure on the throne says deliberately. "I am the prime Shaper of your Test, and I deem this necessary! I am Fistandantalus, and you must now stand in judgment before me!" Turn to **163**.

16

Something in the riddle clicks in your mind. *Is this real,* you ask yourself, *or merely an illusion!*

Once again your years of training at the magic school prove their worth. An illusion it is, but a deadly one—one that could kill you. You realize that Par-Salian and his long-dead colleagues are deadly earnest.

With the ground rushing up at you, you close your eyes and concentrate. You clear your mind of everything but the thought of being on solid ground.

Turn to **141**.

The door with the black triangle stands before you. It's made of a metal you've rarely seen on Krynn. It looks like smooth, burnished steel—a whole door of it! This door would be worth a fortune if you could get it outside of the Towers!

Come back to reality, you chide yourself. You have far more important things to consider than the price of steel in Krynn.

You reach for the door handle and turn it cautiously. It gives with a soft click, but the door doesn't swing open. In fact, nothing happens at all—right away.

But as you attempt to release the handle, you find that your hand is locked in place. Try as you will, you can't get it loose! Even worse, the handle is starting to get cold—very cold! You struggle to free your hand from the door handle as the cold begins to freeze your hand. Frost begins to form on your hand and starts to spread its numbing coldness up your arm and into your chest. You continue to jerk and pull, frantic to get free. Finally you pull out your dagger, intending to cut yourself loose if need be, but it's too late! The cold envelops your chest and surrounds your heart, slowly tightening on it until it ceases to beat.

As you drop to the ground, your mind screams one last plaintive thought: *NO! This can't be! It can't end now, not like this. How could I have been so—*

Turn to **18**.

The stone inner chamber of Par-Salian is silent, as if the ancient stones are waiting for some arrival.

Abruptly the silence is broken by the sound of approaching steps, accompanied by the rattle of armor. Through the door steps a tall young warrior. He has been waiting impatiently for this moment and strides forward anxiously.

The great mage, seated on his throne, watches as the warrior approaches. He regrets the news that he must now give to Caramon. When the warrior finally reaches the throne, a look of dread covers his young face.

"I—I came when I heard your summons, sir," Caramon

stammers. A gut-level fear causes his usually strong voice to tremble. "What news is there of my brother? Has he completed his Test? When can I see him?"

The mage looks down at a bundle of red cloth in his lap for what seems like an eternity. Finally he glances up to the young warrior. *Short will be kinder,* he thinks sadly.

"I will not burden you overlong, Caramon. Your brother will not be going home with you. He has failed. You will have to take home what is left of his effects. For what it may be worth, you have my condolences. Try to understand that, for reasons of our own, we feel his loss as deeply as you." He places the bundle at the foot of his throne.

With trembling hands, Caramon reaches up and takes the small red bundle of Raistlin's robe. He pulls the bundle to his great chest, holding it tightly. As great sobs begin to wrack his body, he collapses to his knees and rocks slowly back and forth, cradling his brother's last remnants like a small child. Finally he struggles to his feet and turns to leave.

The sight is too much for the ancient mage. With tears of compassion in his own eyes, he weaves a spell of consolation around the retreating warrior, a light geas that will allow him to continue to live while bearing in his heart the memory of his brother.

But even as the young warrior leaves the hall, a great, soul-wrenching wail tears free from his shattered soul, echoing endlessly through the Towers of High Sorcery.

As Caramon's cry of despair washes over Par-Salian, the nether voice speaks to the ancient mage once again. If anyone other than the mage could have heard the voice, he would have sensed a note of dread in it.

"It appears that our 'sword' has broken after all," it whispers. "What now?"

Par-Salian sits and ponders silently for a moment. So much had depended upon the young mage. So much would now have to be done. So much to do in so little time. At last he breathes deeply and answers the disembodied voice.

"We will have to seek another," he says softly. "Let us fervently hope that we find him before the world itself is destroyed!"

You realize that your skill is about to be put to the ultimate test! The room is already filling with an inky blackness from the drow's Darkness spell. With its infravision, you know that it can defeat you in that darkness, but you hold your salvation in your hands!

Roll one die and add the result to your agility skill score. If the total is 10 or more, adding whatever experience points you may choose to use, turn to **129**. If it is less than 10, turn to **89**.

If I'm going to save that gully dwarf's life, you think rapidly, *I'll have to attack the one with the whip and its companion. Then I'll deal with the leader.*

Quickly you begin to speak familiar arcane words. You feel the magic forces surge through your body, harnessed by your will, and prepare to erupt.

Turn to **10**. Cross-index the spell you choose to cast with the number of this section. Continue the adventure by turning to the section listed where the two columns meet.

Your jaw drops open in amazement as you look up at the majestic beast standing over you. Its coat is of the purest gleaming gold, and its mane and beard are of a darker golden hue. A single twisted horn protrudes from its forehead. The horn, like its hooves, is of a luminescent golden-pink color.

The beast seems to radiate a light of its own. Its inscrutable violet eyes are full of intelligence and wisdom as they gaze at you.

It is a legendary Ki-rin, a creature of fable.

"Yes, I am what you think I am," it says, its wind-chime voice tinkling in your ears. "It was I who brought you here. You are fortunate to have survived your first encounters. You will note that your wounds have been treated, though you are not up to full strength. That is why you are here—to rest and prepare for the next phase of the Test as best you can."

Unconsciously you run your hands over your body, noticing that the ache of the wounds you suffered during the first day of your Test has lessened. Restore 3 points to your hit point total.

But now this creature speaks of the next phase. You aren't sure if you are ready for it.

Your thoughts are interrupted in midstream by a sudden, frightening realization that causes your stomach to tighten in uncharacteristic terror. As the feeling grows, you frantically begin to rifle through your robe. You search the tiny pockets and pouches hidden there for the all too familiar lumps and bulges of your own spell components.

They're all gone! All of your prized spell components have vanished!

Turn to **65**.

22

Unspeakable terror flails at your mind and body. There is no defense against it. Confused thoughts shriek wildly inside your head and shatter the last remnants of control.

How can this be? you think wildly. *We have been invited! Are we no longer welcome? Have I indeed been too arrogant? Perhaps Caramon should not have come after all. No, that isn't it. It's not his fault. I am to blame; I am unworthy! I don't belong here!*

You turn and run as fast as you can. You trip on a half-buried root and slam headlong into the ground. Sobs of anger and frustration wrack your body. You weep until no more tears come and lie there, not caring, a formless lump on the mist-shrouded path.

After some time, you hear the soft thud of a horse's hooves. They stop beside you, and Caramon's voice reaches through your mind's haze. He is frantic with fear, and you can barely understand him.

"Raist! . . . Raistlin, it's me, Caramon," he whispers quickly. "Please, Raistlin, get up and answer me. We've got to get out of here! Please, Raistlin. Get up and listen to me!"

Slowly you rise to a sitting position. Your brother plops down beside you.

"Raistlin," he stammers, "the hooded man . . . he—he stopped as soon as you ran. He just stood there laughing at you. I tried to stop him, but he lifted his hand again, and I was frozen to the spot! I couldn't move at all, Raist, no matter what I did. I've never been so scared! I couldn't do anything!"

He stops to control himself before he continues. "He looked at me for a while and shook his head. Then he told me I was to give you a message. He said to repeat it exactly, word for word. He said you'd understand why I was to give it to you."

He falters at this point, and you look up at him. His gaze is fixed on the mists as the message he has been magically bound to deliver tumbles from his lips. Turn to **143**.

23

You stare at the silent crowd, waiting for some sort of response to your accusations.

Explosively, it happens. With one collective voice, the mob erupts. They surge against the platform, and several of them clamber up on it, grabbing you roughly by the arms. Then they drag you over to where Verminaard stands waiting.

"What should we do with this unbeliever?" shouts one of your captors. "Surely the new gods don't allow heretics to go unpunished!"

"Indeed not," Verminaard sneers. "The flock has been stained by this heretic. It would appease the gods if the stain were—*burned out!* Tie him to the altar!"

The crowd roars its approval as you are bound to the altar and wood is piled around your feet. Verminaard, with a grim smile on his face, drives a torch deep into the wood, and it bursts into crackling flames. In seconds your robes have begun to burn. The flames begin to scorch your skin, sending excruciating pain through your nerves.

You look one last time at the mob. They seem like animals, watching with an insane sort of rapture as your body begins to crisp and burn. The pain is intolerable, but your frustration at your failure is even more unbearable. You fell into a trap by not learning a lesson from your past.

Now you will pay the supreme price for that failure.

A scream of anguish tears from your lips, answered by shouts of triumph from the crowd. The last thing you hear is Verminaard's cackling, triumphant laughter. Turn to **18**.

24

Well, you think, there's no sense turning back. *Let's find out what lies ahead.*

As you advance cautiously, the tunnel continues to curve. Rounding the bend, you get a clear view of a large chamber at the end of the tunnel. You see a thin post, about the size of a sapling, rising from the sandy floor. A thin gold chain is attached to the post and leads off to a side of the chamber you cannot see from where you are. There's another tunnel opening in the wall opposite where the chain leads.

Then something moves, and you see an ominously large, two-legged shadow moving across the far wall. The shadow raises its head and pounds the air with its fists. The thundering roar splits the air in the tunnel once again.

By sheer force of will, you continue to advance along the tunnel. Suddenly you bump into some sort of barrier. You run your hand carefully up and down the invisible blockade. As you examine it more closely, you see a set of hinges set against the opposite wall. It seems your path is being blocked by a door of some strong, clear material.

Suddenly your heart sinks into your feet. *The door opens outward!* you realize. *Whatever's in there can get to me!*

At that moment, the shadow moves toward the center of the chamber. You watch in frozen terror as the largest, bluest humanoid figure you ever saw appears in the chamber opening.

It towers over you by easily another six feet. The thin gold chain you saw leading from the post in the center of the chamber is attached to a slender golden collar strapped around the creature's neck. Fangs protrude from its mouth, and a single short horn juts out from its forehead. It casts its baleful eyes upon you and shouts something in a language you've never heard before. You know you're going to have to act fast.

Roll one die and add the result to your agility skill score. If the total is 7 or more, turn to **160**. If it is 6 or less, go to **181**.

25

The blazing flame from the fireball spreads out and engulfs you. It's all over!

Suddenly, strangely, all motion stops. The flames cease their raging, and the fiery wind stops whipping at your robes and hair. You stare in wonder across the cavern, through the still flames. The drow stands frozen in time, its hand outstretched, its mouth agape.

You reach out curiously to try to feel whether the flames are still burning and gasp in amazement as you see your hands.

The long, fine fingers glint with a strange metallic golden color. You stare at them, running one hand over the other, then up your arms and to your face. Your whole body seems to be covered with this golden coating! As your hands touch your hair, you realize another difference. You pull a strand of long hair around in front of your face. It's snow white!

In the midst of your amazement, a dusty voice wheezes into your mind. "You see, boy?" whispers Fistandantalus. "Between the two of us, there is nothing we cannot do. This small protection is nothing compared to what we will experience in the future!"

Suddenly the great mage is standing before you. You eye him suspiciously, remembering the thoughts that came to you before the fireball struck.

Returning your gaze, the mage chuckles. "No, you were right, Raistlin. You weren't supposed to be able to win this one. I wanted to see how well you held up against overwhelming odds. How else could I bring you to the point of having to help me? Since you are still alive, you can assume that I am duly impressed with you and your abilities."

He chuckles again. "But enough of that. Look to your enemy. The drow is held for only a short time, but I have taken care of its magic-resistance. If you use the list of spells you found earlier, you will succeed and make it look as though you did it on your own. We wouldn't want to arouse Par-Salian's suspicions, would we?"

If you have the Staff of Magius, turn to **194**. If you don't have the staff, turn to **222**.

26

"I am prepared and will continue with the test, Master Par-Salian." Your reply is full of confidence.

"You have selected and prepared the spells you intend to use during the Test?" Par-Salian asks.

"I have chosen them," you reply.

It is time for you to choose your spells for the first segment of the Test. You may choose two first level spells and one second level spell, as listed in section **10**. After you have chosen your spells, write them on the back of your Character Stats Card and turn to **159**.

27

The journey to Solace doesn't take long. In a short time, you arrive at the edge of town.

Your eyes take in the peaceful village where you grew up. Tall vallenwood trees stand all around you, nestling homes and shops protectively in their great branches. Swiftly you pick out the Inn of the Last Home, a favorite stopping place. Your thoughts leap to your old friends Tanis, Flint Fireforge, Tasselhoff Burrfoot, and other traveling companions. You think of the many pleasant hours you shared with them at the inn. Your mind turns to your half-sister, Kitiara, who was responsible for starting your magic training. *Will I ever see her, or any of them, again?* you wonder.

You notice differences, too. Everything seems much younger and newer, less worn than you remember it. The town hasn't looked this good since you were young.

"Of course!" you whisper. "This is the Solace of my past! 'Mistakes may be forgiven' the voice told me. I wonder which ones. And who are these bullies the sign referred to?"

Suddenly you realize that something else is not right. Your sense of foreboding grows, although there is no apparent reason for it. There are no signs of destruction or obvious changes, yet you feel tension in the air, as though something were about to happen. You have the distinct feeling of being watched, but you see nothing—no birds, no dogs, no people—nothing. The town is as empty and quiet as a tomb.

Turn to **114**.

28

"Kalith karan, tobanis-kar!"

Once again the familiar tingle of magic surges through you. Almost instantly, power rushes into your hands. Two glowing white darts spring to your fingertips and fly toward the monster attacking Caramon.

Both fiery darts strike the beast solidly in the rump. With a yelp of pain, the monster turns to face this new threat.

Gleaming red eyes stare at you in fury. The creature's great maw gnashes the air, anticipating tearing you into bits. Turn to **158**.

29

"Well," Fistandantalus pronounces slowly, "it seems you have made a decent accounting of yourself. Certainly you are to be congratulated for having gotten this far, though some of your reactions could have been better. But that can be cured by time and experience. You made it to this point, and I can still use you!" Turn to **46**.

30

Just as you begin to twist free, Caramon suddenly tightens his grip on your waist.

"No, Raist," he says slowly. "I can't let you do it. If you were to get yourself killed, I'd be lost. I just can't let you do it!"

The next few minutes are a nightmare. All your reasoning, pleading, cursing, and screaming cannot change your brother's mind. He flings you across your horse and ties your hands and feet under its belly. Your screams of frustration echo off the mountain walls, but it's all to no avail. Caramon is determined to take you home, where you will suffer far more than he can ever know. Your attempt to become one of the greatest magicians of your age has come to an ignominious end.

31

With careful concentration, you focus the magic forces of your Charm Person spell on the mind of the lead dragonman. You sense when your mind touches the creature's, your will intertwining with and overriding its own. Soon you know you are in control.

You step from your hiding place and shout to the other two dragonmen, "Stop! Leave that dwarf alone!"

The dragonmen whirl around, the little dwarf forgotten. Cruel-looking short swords appear instantly in their hands as they move to attack.

"Hold it, you louts!" hisses the commanding voice of the leader from across the room. "Don't bother this human. He's one of my trusted friends." The leader moves across the room toward you.

The smaller dragonmen look in puzzlement at you, then

at their leader, then at each other.

"Put down your weapons, I say!" commands the leader.
"Go below and await further orders. Now!"

Startled, they jump into the hole obediently.

"Perhaps you could let the dwarves go, too," you suggest.

"Of course," the lizardlike creature hisses amiably and
strides over to the pot. Grabbing it on one side, it heaves it
over on its side and spills the dwarves onto the floor. They
waste no time scurrying off down one of the tunnels.

The leader smiles at you once more. "Is there anything
else I can do for you?" it asks.

"No . . . I think not," you reply cordially. "It has been good
to see you again. But right now I have a very important
matter to see to. So if you wouldn't mind following your
friends down below, I'll be on my way."

"Of course," it says and dives through the hole.

Suddenly you feel very strange. You look up to see the
walls of the chamber beginning to shimmer with a strange,
iridescent light, as if some powerful magic is at work! Turn
to **123**.

32

Calm, rich, and soothing though Verminaard's voice may
be, you are not taken in by its spell. What he is doing is
clear, and he cannot enthrall you.

You know that he is twisting history to suit his own pur-
poses. You remember well the lessons you learned in your
magic school, lessons that had been drilled into you con-
stantly. If the prideful Kingpriest of Istar had not
demanded of the gods that which they had already freely
given, the Cataclysm would never have taken place. That
was the truth of the matter, but not according to this lying
cleric. His false words assault your senses and set you in a
rage. *Not only does he blaspheme,* you think angrily, *but*

he would rob these people of all they have, including their freedom. I must stop him!

The cleric comes to the end of his harangue, closing with a question that shows how sure he is of his hold over the throng. "How can we do aught but prepare for the coming of the new gods?" he asks. "Who is there that can stand against their mighty power?"

Your anger explodes in a shout. "I can!" you cry loudly. "And I will always stand against deceit and falsehood!"

Your shout resounds over the otherwise silent square. The crowd around you turns and stares dumbly as the cleric immediately spots you in the crowd and glares venomously at you. You push your way toward the platform and climb it purposefully. Then you turn to the crowd to speak.

"How can you let this man fill your heads with this nonsense about new gods? Have you forgotten the history of our land and the mighty power of the gods who shaped Krynn? Are there no singers among you or tellers of the old tales to keep the past alive? What of the 'Canticle of Huma?' The old gods showed their awesome power to Huma and saved Krynn from the ancient evils!"

An uncertain buzz goes through the crowd. Then an angry voice shouts back at you. "Where are your old gods now? They left us to rot after the Cataclysm!"

A woman with a young child in her arms takes up the cry. "What have your old gods done for us lately? They are gone forever! This priest speaks of gods who send messengers to save us. Verminaard himself was sent by the new gods!"

The woman's feelings are echoed by others. Soon the whole crowd is in an angry mood. They shout and scream curses against the old gods and you, their voices full of hate and derision. You see the cleric look at you and smile confidently. He knows he has these people in his control.

From somewhere in your past, the dim recollection that troubled you earlier tries to force its way to the front of your mind.

Roll one die and add the result to your reasoning skill score. If the total is 7 or more, turn to **42**. If it is less than 7, turn to **186**.

33

Too late, you realize that the spell you've chosen is hopelessly wrong for the situation. You try quickly to summon another spell, but your concentration and confidence are shattered.

After watching your feeble magical attempts for a few seconds, the leader of the bullies laughs out loud. "So much for the magic show, fellows," he says shortly. "Let's teach this bumbling fool a lesson!"

You watch fearfully as they quickly close on you. You don't even have time to draw your dagger before you feel blows from fists and clubs pummeling your head and shoulders. Mercifully, one of the clubs smacks your head soundly and you go limp.

Deduct 2 points from your hit point total and turn to **219**.

34

"It appears you're doomed to stay imprisoned here forever," you say. "If you want to believe in something so foolish when I've explained that you are held by nothing more than a thin gold chain and collar, you deserve your fate. It seems that my predecessors were right. You're far too stupid to deserve to escape from your prison."

Turn to **181**.

35

You think you have everything you need to fulfill the Test. There's a Continual Light spell in the Staff of Magius—and you have the staff itself! With those, your spells, and Fistandantalus's help, what more can you need?

Roll one die and add the result to your reasoning skill score. If the total is 9 or more—adding experience points if

44

you choose to spend them—go to **96**. If it is less than 9, choose three spells from your spellbook in section **10**—two first level and one second level—record them on the back of your Character Stats Card, and turn to **199**.

36

You shake off your nagging doubts about the wisdom of entering the wood and say to Caramon, "My sentiments exactly," as you spur your mount toward the forest.

As you approach the ghastly wood, however, you begin to realize that it is far worse than you thought. A palpable uneasiness reaches out to surround you, clawing at your mind and heart. Shadowy shapes of unthinkable things scuttle and slither through the thorny bracken of the wood. Other forms, bent and formidable, shift slowly to and fro in the fog. Disembodied voices speak inside your mind, muttering ceaselessly about things you don't want to know. Thoughts of death and decay pervade your mind. You look to your brother and see his face clouded with fear.

"May—maybe we'd better turn around, Raist," Caramon says in a hushed whisper that betrays his growing terror. "I don't even see a way in."

His fear touches your flagging confidence as you realize he is right. The dense wall of writhing, twisted vegetation blocks your way completely.

Perhaps, you think, *it* would *be better if we left. This could get one or both of us killed.*

Test your reasoning skill here. Roll one die and add the result to your reasoning skill score. Don't forget to add any experience points if you choose to spend them. If the total is 7 or more, turn to **109**. If it is less than 7, turn to **14**.

37

"Well, that's that," you say to yourself. "It looks like they're gone for good. I'd best go see to the gully dwarf."

You march boldly out of your hiding place toward the prone figure on the floor. Your confidence is at a peak now as you silently hope that the Shapers of the Test have taken note of how you handled the dragonmen.

You move over to the gully dwarf and lift her to her feet as she smiles at you adoringly. The gratitude in her eyes warms your heart.

Suddenly her eyes glance past your shoulder. She throws one hand over her mouth and backs away. Taken aback by this sudden change in behavior, you stare at her. Only when a terrified scream leaves her throat do you turn to see what is wrong.

You are looking straight into the glittering eyes of the dragonman leader. You barely have time to shout in surprise before its heavy steel mace crashes into the side of your head, and everything goes black.

Subtract 6 points from your hit point total and turn to **15**.

38

Without hesitation, you intone the words of your chosen spell, gleefully awaiting the downfall of your overconfident opponent.

Your glee disappears at once, however, and you realize the total futility of your actions. Even as the spell passes harmlessly through the air, you know that you cannot defeat him. He has no body to attack!

You are momentarily panic-stricken. How can you fight something that isn't even there?

Before you can attempt to form an answer, the shrouded spectre raises both hands in front of him. Walking slowly in a small circle, he begins to clap. His clapping echoes eerily in the fog and grows louder and louder, as though joined by a distant crowd. You hear the sound of booing and catcalls coming from the mists surrounding you. You begin to feel like some cheap illusionist putting on a sideshow.

The spectre begins to broaden his clapping motions,

exaggerating them extremely. The roaring from the unseen audience grows louder.

You stare about wildly, frantic to put an end to the ridicule being heaped upon you.

Roll one die and add the result to your presence ability score. If the total is 8 or more, turn to **76**. If it is less than 8, turn to **162**.

39

Time, time, time, you think helplessly. *There's never enough of it when you need it most!*

The spell you chose should have been more than adequate, but these ruffians were not at all appreciative of your magical skill. With a short bark from the leader, they swarmed all over you, breaking your concentration.

You feel a thumping blow on your head from a club, and as you fall to the ground, you can only hope they don't beat you to death.

Subtract 2 points from your hit point total and turn to **219**.

40

I've got to keep it off balance, you think desperately. *This ought to do the trick!*

As fast as thought, your Magic Missile spell spills from your lips, and the gleaming darts form at your fingertips and fly at their target. With grim satisfaction, you watch them hit the drow in the head and throat.

The impact slams it up against the far wall, buying you more time—you hope. But the drow simply springs off the wall, with not a wound on it, as though it were never touched by the missiles at all!

A dreadful thought crosses your mind. What if the drow is magic-resistant? Turn to **157**.

41

The sight of your brother lying helpless at the feet of his enemy is more than you can bear. You rush to his side, heedless of the looming spectre. Gently you raise Caramon to a sitting position and offer him what comfort you can, then look up in contempt at the being that has just vanquished your brother.

"Well," you begin, venom dripping from your voice, "have you finished playing your little game with us, or do you have some other surprises in mind?"

At first the spectre does nothing but stand there, observing you. Then the hollow voice speaks once again from beneath the hood.

"Fear not for him, youngster. He will survive; his arm will heal. Be more concerned for yourself! The fact that you did nothing to prevent this injury does not speak well for you or for your chances to survive in the towers. This tardy show of compassion for your brother's suffering is somewhat unexpected. You would do well to make use of those compassionate feelings. Compassion can prove to be a more powerful force in the Test than the most potent of spells."

He pulls a small vial of liquid from his sleeve and hands it to you. "For now, see to your brother's wound. This potion should take care of it. Proceed, then, to the towers, which lie just ahead. Par-Salian awaits within to confer with you. If circumstances permit, you and I may meet again. For now, farewell."

With that, the robed figure turns and vanishes into the mists.

As you administer the healing potion to Caramon, you ponder the minion's words. You are still thinking about them as you and Caramon ride up the path toward the towers. Turn to **69**.

42

Like a bolt from the hand of Paladine, you realize two things almost at once.

Half, perhaps even more, of this false cleric's power comes directly from the people. They want to believe in something, anything, even if it's not true. And secondly you finally remember why this place seems familiar.

Some time ago, during an adventure, you had come into just such a dirty little town as this and confronted a false cleric. You knew he was preying on the despair of the poor and desperate people of the town, so you set about to expose him for the charlatan he was. And you succeeded. But the townspeople were so enraptured by his words and his promises that they wanted to believe him, and you had shattered their hopes. They caught you and placed you in bonds and prepared to burn *you* at the stake instead of the fake cleric. If it hadn't been for your friends, you'd be a dead magician now.

But here you are again, and your experience makes you uncertain what to do. It would be unfair to leave these people under the influence of this fake. Besides, Par-Salian himself specifically warned you not to turn away from any confrontation during the Test. To leave might be a serious mark against you.

Yet what if the reaction of these townspeople is the same as that of the people in the other town? What if they, too, want to believe this false cleric? Is any hope better than no hope at all?

All these thoughts spin through your head in a matter of seconds. But you are still left with the decision to make.

If you feel that you should stand and face the crowd and try to convince them of the error of their ways, turn to **186**. But if you feel you should leave them to whatever fate awaits them at the hands of the cleric and his new gods, turn to **72**.

43

The steel door with the black triangle opens into a wide circular room. Dim light seeps in through a cracked domed ceiling above your head. Fungus, moss, and vines grow through the cracks and cover the walls, giving the place a wild look. Across the room from you stands the statue of a woman carved from blue stone. You don't recognize the face, but it seems to radiate benevolence and warmth. It vaguely resembles one of the old gods, but you can't remember which one.

In front of the statue, you see a large round hole. Peering into the opening, you see a spiral staircase leading down. The stairs are clean and well worn. *Are they still in use,* you wonder, *and if so, by whom?*

Spiraling downward, the stairs lead you to an arched opening. Through the opening, you can see what looks like a great hall. It certainly looks peaceful enough.

As you step out into the large hall, you are shaken to your very boots by the sound of a great gong. Once, twice, three times it sounds, reverberating through the hall as though announcing your presence to the whole world.

"Now what do I do?" you grumble. "That cursed bell has probably alerted every unholy creature around that I'm here!"

Almost immediately you hear voices, grunting and muffled, and the sound of running, scuffling bare feet slapping on stone. The noises are coming from the staircase behind you.

You turn quickly, looking for some place to hide. You notice a dark niche on the far side of the room and quickly conceal yourself as you hear the voices once more, much closer this time.

"The bosses! The bosses are calling!" shout the voices in an almost idiotic, singsong fashion. "Time to go to work! Work, work, work! Hurry up!" The pace of the running quickens as the gong sounds three times again. Turn to **224**.

44

Fingering the tiny chunk of gum arabic enclosing a single eyelash, you feel the magic tingle through your body as your Invisibility spell takes effect. The ogre blinks and rubs its eyes, peering intently in your direction. Finally it takes one step backward and shouts again in a language you do not understand.

Since the ogre is making no move to get you, you have time to cast another spell by turning to **10**. But if this was the third spell you've used and you still haven't learned what the ogre is shouting, turn to **181**.

45

You've never seen a creature this size move so fast! Before you can leap from your mount, the monster crashes into you and knocks you to the ground. Its huge, fearsome mouth instantly locks onto your shoulder, shaking it violently. Blood wells out of the creature's maw . . . your blood! A scream of pain escapes from your throat!

Your scream is echoed by a bellowing war cry. By some miracle, the tearing jaws release their hold on your shoulder. An ear-shattering howl of pain erupts from the beast's mouth, and it topples off you.

You hear another howl, followed by the same war cry—Caramon's! Fighting to keep from passing out, you raise your head. Through pain-clouded eyes, you watch as Caramon's huge sword cleaves the air in a wide arc. It catches the ogredog in the neck, severing its head from its shoulders. Instantly the monster crashes to the ground in a lifeless heap.

Bathed in a fountain of blood, Caramon throws back his head and shouts his victory cry to the hills.

Now that the danger is past, your body finally succumbs to the pain that courses through you and you fade into unconsciousness. Turn to **103**.

46

"As the prime Shaper of your Test," Fistandantalus begins, leaning back in his throne, "I have planned one final trial for you. Par-Salian, as one of the other Shapers of the Test, knows this, but he does not know what it will be. I can assure you it is very difficult—so difficult, in fact, that you will not be able to survive it on your own. Therein lies the root of my proposition.

"I will aid you during the last phase and guarantee that you will live, if you, in return, will grant me a favor."

You are puzzled by his offer. "That's an intriguing proposition, Great One," you reply, "but what can one as humble as I possibly do to help you, the most powerful mage of all?"

"Most powerful?" he says questioningly. "But of course. That is what history has taught you. But I am merely a man, as you can see. To become what history knows me as, I need more than what I am. I need some of the essential life-force of one such as yourself to help me transcend the bonds of mortality and magic. Only then can I find access to the realms of power I seek. In short, Raistlin, I will share your very life. In return, I offer immortality, for you can never die as long as I need you.

"Now time grows precious, young mage. You have heard my proposition. Aid me, share with me a portion of your life-force, and be guaranteed victory in the Test. Reject me, and you must face the final ordeal on your own."

If you choose to accept Fistandantalus's offer and have at least 5 experience points left, turn to **149**. If you choose to accept his offer but have only 3 or 4 experience points remaining, turn to **8**. If you have fewer experience points or choose to reject his offer entirely, turn to **170**.

47

"That's enough of selecting components for right now," you say aloud to yourself. "I'm really famished. I'd better get to that meal before the food gets cold. I'll find the rest of the components I need during the next phase of the Test."

You sit down to a wonderful meal. The food is more than enough to fill you, and you soon drift off to sleep. Turn to **150**.

The Ki-rin is diving straight toward you, but judging by its graceful and unhurried approach, you stand your ground without fear. It doesn't appear to be attacking you.

As it comes to rest on the ground in front of you, you manage to close your gaping mouth and speak. "Am—am I to understand," you ask hesitantly, "that you are the creature that's supposed to 'happen along' here? I—I still can't believe I'm seeing this!"

The creature's deep violet eyes regard you distantly. "Believe it, young master," says the Ki-rin, its smooth and melodious voice accompanied by the tinkling sound of wind chimes. "You have completed the first phase of your Test. Now you are called back for rest in preparation for the next phase. Par-Salian has asked that I take you on the return trip to the plane of the towers."

You are stunned as the magnificent beast drops to one knee to let you mount. To your knowledge, no one has ever ridden such a wondrous creature before. Hesitantly, almost as if in a dream, you climb to its back.

Immediately the magnificent beast leaps into the air, nearly throwing you from its back. Before you realize it, you are galloping through the sky. Images of strange, unknown landscapes and starscapes pass by swiftly as you travel the planes separating you from the towers.

In an incredibly short time, you see the Towers of High Sorcery looming beneath you. Instead of landing in the courtyard, the Ki-rin continues to fly straight toward the inner tower. The tower walls loom closer and closer, until it is clear that your strange mount is going to fly right into them!

Surely the Shapers of the Test are intent upon killing me! you think desperately.

At the last minute, you throw your arms up in front of your face and utter a silent prayer to Gilean as the beast careens into the tower wall. Turn to **134**.

49

You stand paralyzed, unable to move or speak. You know for certain now the nature of the creature you face. That knowledge and the spell the spectral minion has cast have frozen your mind and tongue with dread. You are too frightened to even warn your twin of his deadly peril.

Caramon is aware of only one thing. Danger is approaching. He sees your predicament and responds in the only way he knows. You watch, petrified, as he prepares to fight the spectral minion. You know what the outcome must be. Turn to **113**.

The first beginnings of real fear start to tighten your stomach into knots.

Continual Light? Staff? you think. *I have neither of these spells! Are they necessary to survive this ordeal?*

Something in the back of your mind tells you that without them you are doomed, but your pride and spirit won't admit defeat so easily. You have your training and your spells. They've seen you through so far. They can and will again!

You take a few minutes to consider those spells. Fistandantalus said you would be free to use them. You can only hope that he meant they would come to you as bidden. You sort through them in your spellbook and choose the ones you will use in the next phase of the Test.

Select two first level spells and one second level spell from section **10** and write them on the back of your Character Stats Card.

Your spells selected, you comtemplate your best course of action. You try your best to overcome the fear knotting up your insides. You rise slowly to your full height and stride around the corner into the cavern beyond, but anyone watching might well notice a certain reluctance in your steps. Turn to **199**.

From this point in your adventure until its end, add 1 to all your agility checks. Be sure to note the fact on your Character Stats Card. Fear tends to make one move a little faster than usual!

If you have chosen spells of an offensive nature—Burning Hands, Charm Person, Magic Missile, Push, Sleep, or Web—for this day of the Test, take the left-hand tunnel and go to **118**.

If you chose defensive spells—Hold Portal, Comprehend Languages, Audible Glamer, Darkness 15', ESP, Invisibility, or Mirror Image—take the right-hand tunnel and go to **132**.

If you have selected a mixture of offensive and defensive spells, you are free to choose either tunnel. Good luck!

52

Caramon must be shown that I am committed to this course of action! you think desperately. *A spell ought to do the trick.*

Driven by urgent need, your mind and body respond instantly. With the speed of thought, you begin a spell that will keep him from interfering with your decision.

Suddenly Caramon stops dead in his tracks. You are barely conscious of the surprise and confusion that register on his face, so deeply are you concentrating on your spell. But subconsciously you realize that he knows what you intend to do!

Out of the corner of your eye, you see him gathering his massive body to spring at you. What spell do you choose?

Turn to the Spell Resolution Table at section **10**. Follow the line that lists the spell you want to cast until you come to section **52** (the number of the section you are reading). Then turn to the section listed at the junction of these two columns to discover the effects of the spell you selected.

53

Clutching a lump of wax in one hand, you finish the words of your Audible Glamer spell. *Perhaps,* you think, *a little distraction will get them away from the dwarf.* It is a desperate gamble but one that just may work—if they fall for it.

Just before the dragonman's upraised lash descends, an incredible burst of noise erupts from the mouth of the other tunnel as you create the sounds of shouting and running feet.

"Did you hear that, fellows?" says a booming, illusory voice. "The big, bad lizard calls the helpless little gully girl names. Brave talk from someone who only tackles things half its size! Come on out here, you scaly cowards, and let some real men strip your stinking lizard meat from its bones!"

You create more sounds of shouting and the clashing of swords on shields. The dragonmen spin about to face this new challenge. The two smaller ones whip out short, cruel-looking swords. Pounding its mace on the floor and hissing in rage, the leader leaps toward the noise, followed by the smaller dragonmen, and they all disappear into the mouth of the other tunnel.

Suddenly you feel very strange. You look up to see the walls of the chamber beginning to shimmer with a strange, luminescent light, as if some powerful magic is at work! Turn to **123**.

54

You can barely keep your hands from quivering with excitement as you handle the containers of spell components you find on the shelves along the walls. The opportunity to hold some of the most powerful magic elements on Krynn, to learn their names, feel their ominous potential, is an experience you will never forget.

That is, of course, if I get out of this alive, you think wryly.

A careful examination of the shelves shows you that, among other things far beyond your scope of knowledge, the bottles contain the following spell components:

soot	bits of bone
pepper	bat guano/sulphur balls
bat fur	powdered lime
humus	hen hearts
salt	eyelashes in gum arabic
clay	sesame seeds
incense	phosphorus
fine sand	iron filings
bitumen	powdered diamonds
quicksilver	umber hulk blood
mandrake root	powdered corn extract

With extreme care, you choose the items that you think you will need to cast the spells you know.

Write down your choice of spell components on the back of your Character Stats Card. You may refer to **10** if you wish. Remember that you are limited to only four components in all. Then roll one die and add the result to your reasoning skill score. If the total is 8 or more, turn to **178**. If it is 7 or less, go to **47**.

55

It's clear that your calming voice has a hold on Caramon. You now tighten that hold.

"Caramon," you repeat, "he will not harm us, my brother. He is merely a trial placed before us to see if we would remember who we are and why we are here. Believe me, he will only do us harm if we attempt to harm him."

Your twin lowers his sword arm slowly, then turns and glares at you uncomprehendingly. Softer now, and with deeper intensity, your voice holds him firm.

"Do as I say, Caramon. Stand aside and let him come to me. I will deal with him as the situation demands. You go and get my horse. Go!"

Helpless before the hypnotic effect of your voice, Caramon turns, snorting derisively, and slams his sword back into its scabbard. He then stumps off into the mist to retrieve your steed.

Your antagonist continues to approach. A mere foot in front of you, he stops and gazes at you intently. He radiates a magic so powerful that your knees almost buckle as it plays up and down your person. The hood still hides his face, and the same deep, hollow voice echoes from the depths of its folds.

"It seems that the control you are rumored to possess is not rumor at all, but fact! Excellent, young mage! The Shapers of the Test are greatly pleased with their choice. To control yourself *and* that behemoth of a brother of yours is most commendable. You will need that strength of will, and more, during your ordeal. Maintain it and you might yet survive."

At that, he chuckles softly before he continues. "Yes, I

was merely a test. Had you failed to recognize that, my mission would have been of a different nature and far more unpleasant—for you. As it is, I welcome you to the Towers of High Sorcery. They lie just ahead. Par-Salian awaits within to confer with you."

He turns to go, then hesitates and faces you again.

"Raistlin," he says in a hushed voice, "whether you can believe it or not, I bid you good luck. You will need all the aid you can get to come out of this alive. I advise you to be wise and accept whatever help may be offered to you during the Test. Perchance we will meet again, eh? Farewell—for now."

He turns and vanishes into the mist. As you ponder his cryptic advice, Caramon returns with your horse. You mount and press onward, the path clearing as you approach the towers. Turn to **169**.

56

Two glowing white darts from your Magic Missile spell fly from your fingers. One of them hits the leader of the bullies square in the head, knocking him off his feet into a lifeless heap on the ground. The second strikes the right-hand man as he's about to hurl a club. He, too, drops dead to the ground.

The rest of the bullies stare at you dumbly for a few seconds, then turn and run frantically into the woods.

You look around to make sure that they're all gone when you hear a soft noise behind you. You spin around again, only to see the leader getting to his feet and dusting off his trousers. There isn't a mark on him!

He looks up at your surprised face and smiles broadly. "Well, what did expect from an illusion?" he asks innocently. "Surely you didn't really think you could kill us, did you?" He chuckles. "That was quite an impressive display just now, even if it was a little ruthless for the situation. You might have handled it with more compassion."

"I 'handled' it as I saw fit," you reply coolly. "It was you or me. I was justified in killing you."

"Still," he says, serious now, "the Shapers of the Test are looking for good mage material, not a murderer. You would do well to remember that in the future."

As you ponder his words, you see his attitude change markedly. Suddenly he is all smiles and joviality again.

Subtract 2 experience points and turn to **214**.

57

You move with blinding speed. Before the darkness is complete, the only spell that may save you jumps into your head. In no time, your two magic missiles streak across the cavern, striking the drow squarely in the chest and throat!

The drow's spell is broken and the darkness clears. You can see it sagged against the wall. It should be hurt badly enough to give you time to cast your next spell.

To your dismay, however, the drow looks across at you and smiles! It doesn't seem to be hurt in the least! In fact, there's a glint of amusement in its eye.

Its expression turns to rage and galvanizes its actions. You've never seen anything move so fast! The drow's hand blurs and comes up with the small crossbow that was at its belt. A dart wings its way across the cavern, aimed straight at your heart!

You twist, trying to dodge the missile, and the dart misses your heart but plants itself squarely in your arm.

The shock of impact throws you up against the wall, and you immediately feel sleepy!

The dart was drugged! Turn to **157**.

"All you had to do was explain it to me," he says tightly, breathing hard between clenched teeth. "Just tell me what's going on, will you?"

You kneel beside him. You know you owe him at least a partial explanation.

"All right then," you begin. "This much I will tell you. You know that I am going to face the supreme challenge of my abilities as a magic-user. Well, that Test will take place within the Towers of High Sorcery, and the towers lie somewhere within these woods. That is why I must enter this forest. It is absolutely crucial to my future."

His eyes widen at the mention of the towers. He has heard of them only in tales, but their reputation is legendary.

"Caramon," you continue, "it isn't necessary for you to go in there. The Test is for me alone. But you have been most helpful thus far on our journey, and I'm reluctant to lose your support now. Be that as it may, you are free to leave or stay as you will."

Your brother slowly gets to his feet and turns away from you. His head hangs low, and he stands very still, with his back to you, seemingly lost in thought. You have no idea what he will decide.

After several long moments of silence, he straightens his back and turns around to face you. You are surprised to see that he is smiling broadly. Turn to **182**.

What's wrong with these people? you think angrily. Can't they see the falsehood in his eyes, hear the deceit in his voice? Any fool could see through his lies!

You concentrate more closely on the cleric's words, searching for key phrases and blatant lies that will help you expose this fake to the crowd.

As you listen, however, something peculiar begins to happen. You begin to feel a certain comfort and security in his words. The mellow tones of his voice enwrap your subconscious mind in foggy confusion. But despite that confusion, your whole being seems to take on a warm glow. Slowly, ever so slowly, his words erode all your arguments against him, and the cleric starts to make sense to you.

You shake your head in wonderment. *How can this be?* you think. *All that he says is a lie, yet still I feel that I must believe him. Could it be I who have been deceived all these years? Surely this kindly cleric is speaking the truth!*

The incredible spell that Verminaard has woven to enthrall this town has now captured you.

Turn to **82**.

60

Your spell is ready and the dragonman doesn't stand a chance! You'll turn it into dead meat before it begins to charge.

But instead of charging, your opponent stands frozen in its tracks, looking around in confusion.

Now you see what has stopped the creature. The walls of the chamber are beginning to shimmer with an eerie iridescence, as if some powerful magic force is at work!

Turn to **123**.

61

You aren't a skilled horseman, and the beast is far more than you can handle. It rears in fear and throws you to the ground. Cursing, you fall with an ungraceful thud.

Bruised and badly shaken, you struggle to your feet. Scanning the swirling mists in front of you, your eyes search for the object of the horses' terror. At the same time, you review in your mind the spells you have prepared for the day. Which of them will you need first?

As if summoned by your thoughts, invisible magical forces begin to focus around you. The rich magic flow causes your body to tingle with power.

Your brother continues to struggle with his mount, cursing all the while. His curses fade from your hearing instantly as, almost at the same moment, the power around you crystallizes and you spot the object of your search.

Subtract 1 hit point of damage from your total and turn to **5**.

"Well done, Raistlin!" exclaims the great mage. "Your spell use and ingenuity were nearly perfect. You are indeed the one I seek! We have much to look forward to together." Turn to **46**.

A broad smile spreads over the ruffian's face as you send your Charm Person spell to nestle over his body. You know you have him in the palm of your hand.

"Now, that's more like it," you say. "Why don't you and I just have a little talk?"

"All right," he says amiably. "Let's do that. We're the best of friends, after all. Why are we quarrelling, anyway?"

"I honestly don't know," you reply. "I think it has to do with some trivial misunderstanding from the past. I'm sure we could sort it out if there weren't all these undesirable louts about. Do you think you could send them off somewhere else?"

At that moment, you see a sudden movement over his shoulder. The right-hand man is about to throw a club at you!

Roll one die and add the result to your agility skill score. If the total is 6 or more, go to **155**. If it is less than 6, turn to **69**.

You stand with your head bowed, staring at your feet. The encounter in the forest, the overpowering presence of the towers, and more questions than you can answer well up inside you. You begin to think of how your life will be forever changed by the Test. You wonder if the changes are worth the price you may have to pay. It is all very difficult to sort out.

"Great One, I—I truly don't know," you stammer. "Perhaps I was a bit hasty in my decision to come here. I may not be as prepared as I led you to believe."

The great mage looks at you for a long moment before he speaks. "It is a tremendous burden that you are about to assume, Raistlin," he says. "But your admitted lack of confidence is not a good sign. Many before you have expressed the same anxieties at the outset of their trials. Many of them proceeded anyway. Their fates I will not relate to you. You are a powerful young magician, and we can hope that your inner strength will help you overcome your weakness of resolve. But in all honesty, to proceed—especially under such circumstances—could mean your death. The choice is up to you."

If you decide to continue and face the Test now, turn to **26**. If you decide to leave, in hope of getting another chance someday, go to **130**.

65

You are about to tear your empty robe into little bits in an attempt to find your missing spell components when the sound of wind chimes fills the air. The Ki-rin's melodious voice interrupts your frenzied thoughts.

"I have brought you back to the Towers to give you time to rest and eat," it says.

Even as he mentions food, a sumptuous meal materializes on a low table floating in midair in front of you. The table floats to one side of the room and settles gently near a narrow door in the wall.

"Food!" you gasp almost hysterically. "How can I think of food at a time like this? Don't you realize I've lost all my spell components? How can I possibly face the rest of the

Test without them? I'm doomed!"

"Do not bother yourself about that," replies the Ki-rin, with an apparent lack of concern for your predicament. "Your loss is an unfortunate side-effect of our passing through the planes to the towers.

"You no doubt know what this room is used for," he continues. "It is part of your Test to find, among all the magical items here, the ones that you can use in your spell casting. You will be limited in your choices to only four components. Search the room carefully, and choose wisely. After you have done this, you will be given sufficient time to eat, rest, and prepare yourself for the next phase of the Test. When you feel you are ready, pass through yonder portal. It leads to the Corridor of the Doors. The doors will lead to your next trial. Good fortune, young mage."

Immediately the Ki-rin leaps into the air and disappears through the ceiling, leaving the faint tinkling of wind chimes fading behind him.

It looks like it's time to attend to my immediate needs, you think. Turn to **54**.

66

As you travel through the eerie, still forest, your twin's deep voice breaks the deathly silence.

"Is there no end to this miserable fog?" Caramon grumbles. "And what sort of trail is this, anyway? It's barely wide enough for the horses, let alone for any fighting. I swear those little thorny trees have eyes. Probably hiding more foul beasts, or some sorcerer waiting to roast us to death."

True to his nature, Caramon has kept constant vigil since you entered the Wayreth Forest, searching the mists and shadows for any sign of danger.

You chuckle suddenly. "Be at peace, Caramon, and take your hand off your sword hilt. Remember, if we harm nothing, we will get through this wood unscathed."

Your words don't help his mood to improve. "We shouldn't have entered it in the first place," he grumbles. "I've been in lots of dangerous places before, but nothing to equal this."

Your eyes scan the forest that seems to entomb you. "The guardians of the forest won't bother us," you repeat, keeping an eye on the deformed shapes keeping pace with you as you move through the forest.

Suddenly, as though the very air around you has responded to Caramon's sense of foreboding, a chill surrounds you. It feels as if you've just ridden through a wall of ice. You draw your robes more tightly about you and nudge your horse closer to your brother's. The passing wave of cold has sparked some dim, disturbing memory. As you start to mention it to your brother, he speaks again, interrupting you.

"I still don't think we should be here. After all, it was mages who invited us," Caramon grunts. "I'll never trust 'em!"

His comment forces all other thoughts from your mind. You glance at him and ask softly, "Does that include me, dear brother?"

He says nothing but merely hunches back into his saddle and resumes his wary vigil.

He is intent on protecting me, you think bitterly, *as he has throughout my entire life. Would that he could just realize that I am perfectly able to . . .*

Your mind is yanked back to reality by the terrified neighing of a horse. You look up to see Caramon's mount rearing up on its hind legs. You stare in surprise as it paws the air in front of it, as if it's trying to strike an unseen enemy. Your brother struggles gamely to maintain control. Before you can go to his aid, your own horse shies violently away from the path.

Roll one die and add the result to your agility skill score. If the total is 8 or more, turn to **211**. If it is less than 8, go to **61**.

66

67

As Fistandantalus's voice fades, time begins to flow once more. But you are now protected from the raging fire of the drow's fireball, and the flames wash harmlessly around you. As they pass, your plan of attack galvanizes.

You pull the Continual Light scroll from your robes. Reading its words, you feel the power gather around you, then send the power arcing across the room, where it bursts into brilliant sunlight!

It explodes right in the eyes of the drow, dissipating the darkness and blinding your enemy. The drow slumps to its knees, clawing at its eyes as they literally burn in its head.

Offering no quarter, you press the attack, throwing your magic missiles with a vengeance. The gleaming white darts crash into the drow's head and throat, and it slumps, unconscious, against the wall.

You walk across the chamber to where the drow lies. Standing over it, you see its chest rise and fall rapidly. Its face is scarred and bleeding. You pull out your dagger to finish it off.

Suddenly there is a blur, and you barely see a glint of metal before you feel the shock of impact and a searing pain. Something wet and warm seeps down your side. You look down to see the hilt of a drow dagger sticking between your ribs.

Your enemy looks up at you with a wicked grin on its dark face. That was its last act, and it will take you with it into death. As you crumple to your knees, you lash out with your own dagger. The drow is too weak now to do anything about it. You bury it to the hilt deep in its throat. Turn to **73**.

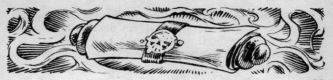

You know that your choice of spells could be dangerous. In order for it to work, you will have to move much closer to the ogredog and get its attention.

But you have no time to worry about that now. Caramon has captured the monster's full attention, but he can't hold it forever. It's time for you to go into action.

Arcane words form on your lips, gathering powerful magical forces. You feel the magic gathering around you. In an instant, three more exact images of you appear. As you draw your dagger, the images draw theirs. In unison, four Raistlins move forward, waving their arms and shouting wildly. It is essential to distract the ogredog, even for a split second.

Surprised to see a whole group of foes, the monster roars a challenge and spins about to face this new threat.

You continue to wave your arms and shout, just out of the creature's reach. The beast is obviously confused. By some uncanny instinctive ability, however, it manages to single you out from among the images. The creature's eyes narrow to slits, and its red orbs change to mere pinpoints of light. Slowly, its teeth grinding in anticipation, it begins to stalk toward you. Turn to **158**.

69

There is no time to dodge. The club catches you squarely in the ribs, and you feel one of them snap as you fall to your knees.

The gang leader stares at you for a moment. Then the smile disappears from his lips as he reaches down to pick up the club. He's frowning as he turns to face his right-hand man. Your heart sinks at his words.

"Thanks, Rafe," he says. "I thought he might try something like that." He turns slowly to face you again. A glint in his eyes tells you he is no longer under your spell.

"Now, Raistlin," he begins, "I've had enough of your trying to make the fool of me. Me and my buddies are going to give you a lesson you'll never forget!"

You watch helplessly as he raises the club over his head and smashes it into your skull. As you collapse to the ground, you feel more blows raining down on your head and body. In moments, you are beaten senseless.

Subtract 3 points from your hit point total and turn to **219**.

70

The fear that has tried again and again to dominate you rises to new intensity, crushing your confidence.

"No!" you whisper. "I will not—I cannot—enter these towers!"

To your amazement, the runes, the gates, the towers—everything around you begins to disappear! It seems to melt into the ground itself. Soon all that is left is a grassy valley floor that stretches out before you. The wind whispers softly through the grass as it passes.

Suddenly, as from a great distance, the voice of Par-Salian, master of all mages, speaks from the air around you. Turn to **210**.

71

You know you will only be able to stop one of the smaller dragonmen with this spell, so you choose the one wielding the whip. *This ought to teach that beast not to mistreat helpless creatures.*

You blow grains of powdered brass from your palm and point your finger at the unsuspecting dragonman. With a shout of surprise, it drops its whip as the force of your Push spell tumbles it all the way across the hall toward the hole in the floor. With a scream, scrambling desperately for a hold at the edge, it rolls through the hole and disappears.

Chaos erupts in the room. The gully dwarves take full advantage of the confusion. Whooping and shouting, they pour out of the pot. The remaining smaller dragonman runs toward the pot, vainly trying to corral the fleeing dwarves.

"Leave them, you idiot!" shouts the leader. "Just glide down below and try to make sure that fool doesn't land on anyone important when he hits the streets. Something is amiss here, and I'm going to find out what it is."

The smaller dragonman dives through the hole. Eyeing the two tunnels suspiciously, the leader begins to dig for something in its belt pouch. It pulls out a small object and moves to the edge of the hole. Then, mumbling something, it steps through the hole and disappears.

Roll one die and add the result to your reasoning skill score. If the total is 8 or more, turn to **146**. If it is less than 8, turn to **37**.

72

As you gaze out over the shouting crowd, Par-Salian's words come clearly to your mind. "Your ultimate success will depend to a great degree on how well you use your experience to see you through your trials," he had said. This is clearly one of those times.

You suddenly realize that you've made the same error that nearly cost you your life in the previous encounter. You had pushed your beliefs on the townspeople then, with no concern for their feelings. That must not happen again. Raising your hands to get the crowd's attention, you pitch your voice to carry through the uproar.

"Very well, then," you shout. "I will leave you to your new gods. May they bring you the joy and hope you seek!"

Your sudden reversal catches the crowd by surprise. You leap from the platform and make your way through the stunned throngs of people.

At last you come to the town gate. *Perhaps,* you think, *at some future time they will learn. I only hope it won't be too late. . . .*

Your thoughts are interrupted by a shout. Startled, you turn to see the captain of the guard running up the street toward you. He stops just in front of you and looks at you approvingly before he speaks.

"I'm supposed to let you know that you did well back there," he says. "I'm also supposed to tell you that you're to go on to Solace—something about 'taking the rest of your

71

Test.' But if you've already been there, you should wait right here. No telling what might happen along."

As he turns and starts back down the street, his body oddly begins to melt into the street until finally he is gone. An illusion!

If you have not yet faced your trial in Solace, turn to **95**. If you have already been to Solace, remain right where you are and wait to see what "happens along" by turning to **131**.

73

You realize that the drow, in its final act, has dealt you a mortal blow. How can one celebrate victory in death? As your blood seeps from your body, you slip into a strange state of nothingness somewhere between life and death—and there Fistandantalus finds you again.

"How foolish of you," he says slowly, "to approach so close to an enemy without knowing it is dead. How very foolish! If you were anyone else, I would leave you to your death. But I cannot. You are integral to my plans and to the fate of Krynn. Therefore, you must be preserved!"

A shadowy hand passes before your eyes. You feel new life entering your being, and you begin to breathe more easily. The tearing pain in your ribs subsides.

"Rise, Raistlin!" says Fistandantalus. "It appears we need to talk again!"

Turn to **189**.

74

"Don't worry yourself on that account, brother," you croon in reply, your voice filled with reassurance. "Even though the Wayreth Forest is brimming with guardians, their mission is to keep out uninvited intruders. We have been invited; therefore we are safe. Harm nothing and nothing will harm you."

Caramon gazes at you for a short while, then stands and walks slowly toward you. Turn to **182**.

75

When you come to, you are lying on the floor of the corridor. Your robes are still covered with a thin layer of frost, and your bones and joints ache from the cold, but you're still alive! As you rise slowly to your feet, a dusty voice speaks softly inside your mind.

"Foolish boy, will you never learn? I am not in the habit of giving assistance only to have it cast aside. Consider again my message. And this time, do not be so foolhardy."

Subtract 2 points from your hit point total, then return to **125** and choose again.

76

Somehow, from somewhere in your inner reserves, you find the strength to step back and analyze what is happening.

You face a foe who now knows you cannot defeat him, yet he continues to taunt you. Why? Even as you reflect, the fire of your rage begins to cool and your inner strength takes over. Slowly the power of reason enwraps your roiling mind and calms you.

No, you declare silently, *I've been a fool. This is not the way I should handle this. The fight will end here!*

Seeing your hesitation, the shrouded figure stops. It is as though he knew of your mental battle and was awaiting the outcome.

Your thoughts return to the situation at hand. The spectral minion stands before you, waiting. Suddenly, in uncharacteristic humility, you bow your head and speak to him.

"Revered stranger, you have defeated me. I will fight you no more, nor can I. If I have not destroyed any chance to face the Test through my insolence, and if you are possessed of any degree of mercy at all, I ask that you accept my apology for my rash behavior."

The figure before you nods in silent approval. Then he speaks. "Raistlin, you are a complex young mage. This sudden show of humility was unexpected. It speaks well of you that you can exercise that kind of control over your emotions. No doubt this will serve you well in the Test.

"But," he continues, "your earlier loss of control bespeaks a weakness that could mean your death in the Test. Therefore, I must share with you a lesson. Look upon me, young mage, and see what your future holds!" Turn to **145**.

77

The sand you collected from the workshop falls silently through your fingers as you softly utter the words of your Sleep spell. As the magic gathers to do your bidding, you send it across the room to engulf the lead dragonman.

Roll one die. If you roll a 1, turn to **206**. If you roll 2 through 6, turn to **4**.

78

Fatigue from your trial and your full stomach finally catch up with you. Wearily you lie down on a low cot in the corner of the workroom to rest. As you doze off, thoughts of the ransacked shelves keep running through your mind. *What if someone else really is using this room when I'm not here?* you think sleepily. *And what if whoever it is comes back while I'm asleep?* You decide there are too many 'what ifs' for your taste. You'll face up to that if it happens.

Finally you slip off to sleep. Add 1 hit point to your total because of the rest you are getting and turn to **112**.

79

That face—the face of your future—shakes you to the quick. *Is anything worth enduring that kind of suffering?* you ask yourself.

The answer comes to you immediately. It resounds through your mind in a flash. *Of course it is—anything for magic. Even that fate is worth it! I will face the Test!*

As though reading your thoughts, the spectre speaks. His voice sounds almost pleased. "So be it, then. Your path is decided. I admire your courage, young mage. You may indeed be the one we have waited for, the one we hoped you would be. Your courage and determination will stand you in good stead during your trial. Use it, cling to it, and you will survive."

His voice drops to an urgent tone. "I must warn you once more that the vision you have seen of your future will hamper you in the Test. Only your inner strengths can help you overcome that obstacle. Go now. The towers lie just ahead. Par-Salian awaits within to meet with you."

He turns and vanishes into the mists. His cryptic words about being 'the one waited for' perplexes you. You are still thinking about them as you mount your horse and ride toward the Towers of High Sorcery.

Turn to **169**. However, from now until the end of this adventure, unless otherwise directed, you must subtract 1 from all your presence skill die rolls because of the vision you have seen of your future.

80

The door with the black triangle seems to draw you toward it. As you approach it, you notice that it is made of burnished steel, a metal that is extremely rare on Krynn. This single door would be worth a fortune if you could somehow get it outside of the towers.

Time to come back to reality, you chasten yourself. You know you have far more important things to think about than the price of steel in Krynn.

You reach for the door handle and turn it slowly. You hear a soft click, but the door doesn't swing open, and you can't seem to push it open, either. In fact, nothing at all happens—right away.

But as you attempt to release the handle, you find that your hand is somehow locked in place. Try as you might, you can't remove it! What's worse, the handle is suddenly getting cold—very cold!

Soon the spreading cold begins to freeze your hand! You strain your muscles, trying to get your hand to open to open and release the knob, but it won't move! Your insides tighten with fear as frost starts to form on your hand! Then a numbing coldness begins to spread up your arm and into your chest! You try frantically to get free from the bitter, stinging cold, but to no avail.

Swiftly the cold spreads through your chest and surrounds your heart. You can feel your heartbeat slowing to a mere crawl as the cold begins to spread to your head and brain. Now even thought becomes difficult. You realize now that you have gone to the wrong door, but that thought doesn't help much.

Finally you drop to the ground, unconscious. Turn to **75**.

"At least this riddle makes a little sense," you mutter. "By 'giving,' the writer obviously means dealing out punishment—being on the offensive. 'Receiving' must mean being on the defensive."

Swiftly the significance of the poem comes to you. If one has chosen to bring along offensive spells, he should go to the left. But if he's chosen defensive spells, then it would be better to go to the right. But what is the nature of the trials that await down these tunnels?

You stand lost in thought, evaluating the nature of the spells you've chosen. Turn to **51**.

Calm reassurance washes over you. *At last,* you think, *a true cleric, one who surely must possess the powers of healing.*

Verminaard continues to preach. His words sound so reasonable, so true, that you cannot help but believe him. You make your way to the front of the crowd, directly beneath the platform.

The cleric finally comes to the end of his sermon and asks, "Who among you will be the first to allow the new gods to demonstrate their power? Who will step forth and demonstrate his faith?" He is looking directly at you.

You are so completely convinced that the new gods are the salvation of Krynn that you leap immediately to the platform, eager to show Verminaard the depth of your conviction.

"Will the new gods accept me?" you ask eagerly.

Verminaard smiles at you. "A newcomer has come to our humble village," he announces to the crowd. "Well, faith is not limited to just we few, and this young man obviously has great faith. May the new gods use him to demonstrate their power by saving him gloriously from death in the flames."

You let yourself be led over to the altar and bound to it. You fail to notice the glint of evil anticipation in Verminaard's eyes as the knots are tied.

Next wood is piled around your feet. The cleric, mutter-

ing some incantation, buries a sputtering torch deep in the wood at your feet. You hear the wood crackle into life, and flames begin to rise around you. Smoke begins to cloud your vision, but your mind is filled only with the power of the new gods and the miracle they are about to perform to save you.

Surely they won't let me die here, you think. *Their power and my faith will preserve me from the flames.*

The fire now spreads to your robes, igniting them and creeping slowly up the fabric, but you are not concerned. You will show everyone that the power to heal has finally returned to the world of Krynn.

Suddenly pain begins to scourge your nerves. Your eyes see the swirling, raging fire burning around you, and your mind snaps out of its thralldom. Through the roar and crackle of the bonfire that is now feeding on your robes and body, you hear the cleric Verminaard shouting to the crowd.

"The new gods know the difference between a true believer and a heretic!" he screams. "This is the fate of the faithless!" The crowd howls its consenting reply as the flames lick at your robes, your hair, your face.

This can't be happening! you shriek silently. *How could I have fallen into his trap? It can't end here! I mustn't die so ignominiously!*

But your thoughts are never heard by the crowd. Verminaard's wicked chuckle penetrates your hearing through the roar of the flames. A scream of pain and heart-rending agony leaps from your throat, and the crowd echoes your scream with a roar of approval.

Turn to **18**.

83

Never has a mistake been more disastrous. The spell you chose doesn't hinder the drow at all! In fact, it gives it all the time it needs to press its own attack! Turn to **3**.

84

Without a spell, you haven't got much to fight with, but you've got to do something or the monster will tear your brother limb from limb!

You search around frantically for some weapon that you may be able to use against the beast. You see a large, heavy tree branch lying on the ground nearby. *That will have to do,* you think, and you rush to pick it up.

With more courage than brains, you spring toward the monster. Raising the club high over your head, you bring it down on the beast's tail with all your strength.

Howling in rage, the creature spins around. One of its huge paws lashes out and smashes you to the ground some ten feet away. Then the beast advances toward you, its red eyes glowing and teeth gnashing. Subtract 2 hit points of damage from your total hit points and turn to **158**.

85

Par-Salian's chamber disappears before your eyes, and you find yourself in darkness blacker and thicker than any you have ever experienced. Somehow it seems to have weight and substance—as though you could reach out and touch it. It squeezes in on you, holding you like a giant hand. You feel an uncomfortable chill in the air, and you begin to wonder if the Test will end right here, with you frozen into a human icicle.

In answer to your thoughts, a small voice enters your brain. It speaks softly from the blackness that enfolds you and fills your mind with a harsh, gasping whisper.

"No, young mage," wheezes the dust-filled voice, "you are not merely to be frozen for our entertainment. Too much awaits you . . . too much depends on you. You will have all the opportunity in the world to prove yourself. Know that some of us have taken a personal interest in your case. We will be watching and waiting, ready to help should the need arise and you choose to accept our aid."

You are amazed to think that someone or something would interfere in your Test, but your thoughts turn immediately to Par-Salian's warning. Could this be the being he spoke of? And why is he offering to help you in your ordeal?

"Who are you?" you ask softly. "What do you want of me, and what do you mean by 'too much depends on' me? Show yourself so that I can see you. I believe I am entitled to an answer to my questions."

Roll one die and add the result to your presence skill score. Subtract 1 from the die roll if you saw the spectral minion in the Wayreth Forest. If the total is less than 9, turn to **165**. If it is 9 or more, turn to **173**. Remember, if you feel it's important enough, you may spend 1 or more experience points.

86

". . . kalith koran, tobanis kar!"

You finish the words of your Magic Missile spell, and two glittering darts of white light form at the ends of your fingertips. As you focus your concentration, they streak across the room and strike the lead dragonman in the throat. Stunned, it's knocked backward by the force of the attack. It drops its mace and clutches its throat, gagging and spitting up blood. Partially blind with pain, the creature stumbles and falls into the pot among the gully dwarves. They waste no time taking out their pent-up wrath on their helpless tormentor.

But the added weight is too much, and the pot immediately begins to sink rapidly through the hole. In a moment, it is out of sight, and the only things you hear are the whoops of angry gully dwarves and screeches of pain from the dragonman.

The two remaining dragonmen stand looking at each other for a second, then glance swiftly in the direction the missiles came from. Finally they look at the hole their leader just disappeared through.

With a shriek, they bolt for the hole. Extending their wings, they dive through it after the pot.

Suddenly you feel very strange. You look up to see the walls of the chamber beginning to shimmer with a strange, iridescent light, as if some powerful magic is at work! Turn to **123**.

87

These mindless dolts should be easy to bluff, you think confidently.

Speaking in as menacing a tone as you can muster, you say, "So you're going to 'get me,' hmm?" You lock their leader's gaze with your most chilling glare. Slowly you turn toward each of them in turn, fixing each squarely in the eye in a brief contest of wills.

"Before you embark on such a foolish undertaking," you warn evilly, "be warned! I have studied the magic arts and have fought many foes since we last met. Many of them were more formidable than all of you combined. I give you fair warning not to continue this fight. It will mean dire consequences for all of you!"

Suddenly you whirl to face the leader and rise to your full height. "And especially to you," you say evenly, thrusting your finger in his direction. "You will be the first to fall!"

Trying your best to keep your hand from shaking, you again lock glares with the leader of the ruffians in an attempt to stare him down.

Roll one die and add the result to your presence skill score. If the total is 7 or more, turn to **13**. If it is less than 7, go to **201**. Remember to subtract 1 from your die roll if you saw the face of the spectral minion in the Wayreth Forest.

88

Another wave of fear sweeps over you, nearly knocking you to your knees, but somehow you are able to withstand it, and you prepare to cast your spell.

This second magical attack, though, proves to be too much for Caramon. From the corner of your eye, you see that he is totally paralyzed, stricken by a terror beyond description. The hooded figure brushes by him and continues to advance toward you. Turn to **119**.

89

You're too late! Utter and complete darkness enfolds you, and you know you are lost!

You stumble backward, trying to find the tunnel you entered the chamber through. Instead, you back into the solid rock wall of the cavern. You forget everything but the impending doom you hear at the other end of the cavern. Frantically you clamber along the wall to find an escape route.

Suddenly a light flares behind you, and you turn to see a thin finger of flame rocketing through the dark. It strikes you in the chest and explodes into a fireball!

If you received either the staff or the scroll, turn to **166**. If you received neither, turn to **12**.

90

As Caramon holds the ogredog's attention, you reach into one of the hidden pockets of your robes and pull out a small handful of sand. The sand trickles from your fingers as the ancient words of the Sleep spell roll from your lips: *"Ast tasarak simularan krynawi."*

Magic fills the air around you, forming a bubble of power. At your mental command, the bubble lifts from the ground and settles over the ogredog.

But nothing happens!—at least, not what was supposed to happen. Instead of falling into a deep sleep, the beast howls in rage and lunges toward your brother. One of its huge clawed paws slashes out and knocks Caramon to the ground. Then the monster whirls about and faces you!

Slowly it begins to stalk you, almost toying with you. Its great teeth grind back and forth, as if in anticipation of tearing you to bits.

Can Caramon recover before this creature tears me apart? you wonder desperately. Turn to 158.

91

I wonder if the table has been rummaged over, too, you think. *Let's have a look.*

Moving to the table, you quickly scan its contents. The little burner and the pail of coal still rest on the table, but you notice that the vase of roses has been tipped over and some of the roses stripped of their petals. The bag of copper pieces that was sitting on top of the parchment is gone, too. You also see that a partially ground rod of brass lies beside the small grinding wheel. The wheel itself is faintly dusted with a coat of finely ground brass powder.

Lying off to one side of the table, seemingly cast aside, is an amber rod partially covered by a strip of bat fur, the unmistakable components of a Lightning Bolt spell. *Too bad I don't know that one,* you think enviously. *It might come in handy.*

Looking under the table reveals the same tiny drum and spiderwebs.

If you think you can use anything you see on the table as a spell component, add it to your list of spell components—but remember to choose no more than four in all. Then turn to 78.

92

As the ground rushes up at you with ever-increasing speed, you curse the dust-filled voice. The riddle is no help at all. The only thing that fills your mind is the assurance that you are a dead magician.

The vision of your smashed body lying on the cobbles of the courtyard below fills your eyes. *This can't be happening!* you scream silently. *What sort of test is this? No . . . no! Don't do this to me, please!*

The scream that tries to escape your throat remains forever silent as you plummet into the tower courtyard, and darkness enfolds you once more. Turn to **200**.

93

As you step off the dais that supports the altar, you hear a soft snapping sound from somewhere below you. Startled, you jump aside and stare at the floor. *What in the name of Gilean could that have been?* you wonder.

Suddenly your thoughts are interrupted by a loud grating sound, like stone grinding against stone. You look up to see the opening that you entered through being sealed by a sliding stone door. Then the floor at your feet slowly begins to rise, carrying you toward the ceiling of the chamber! You're going to be crushed between the floor and the ceiling unless something can be done to stop the movement—and quick! Turn to **139**.

94

Morning brings a rude awakening.

"Raistlin! Hey, Raist! You'd better wake up and take a look at this!"

"Not now, Caramon," you mumble groggily. "It's too early and I'm too tired." You roll over in your blankets. Your warrior brother has been jumpy ever since your arrival in this secluded valley in the Kharolis Mountains the previous evening. No need to pay him any heed now.

The night's sleep had again proved to be insufficient. No one night's sleep could possibly relieve the soul-wearying fatigue caused by the last leg of your quest. The rocky mountain passes and steep trails you traveled through the Kharolis Range were particularly unforgiving. You and your twin brother, Caramon, spent three long weeks of your month-long journey from your home village of Solace wandering their unrelenting, bone-bruising heights. The

Cataclysm and the passing of the old gods from Krynn had done more than strip the world of the true power of healing. It had shattered the land itself, and these bitter mountains were proof positive of that.

Your brother, you must admit, had been of considerable help during the journey. Though he had not really been invited, his skills as a fighter had come in handy. There were creatures abroad in the land that only a warrior of his strength and skill could handle, and you had run into your share of them during your journey. Several times your spells and his sword had barely saved your skins. There is no doubt that you fought well together. If the truth were known, you were actually glad he had come along. It had made a difficult journey whose end could well prove to be deadly that much easier.

Last night you finally reached the secret valley you had sought for so long. You arrived with time to spare, as well. The constellations of the Warrior and the Queen of Darkness had barely begun their eternal contest for the night sky. *Yes,* you thought, *there's plenty of time—time to rest, or perhaps to meditate. . . .* And you certainly needed to collect your spells for the forthcoming Test.

You would soon find out that no such rest was forthcoming.

Again Caramon's frantic shouting intrudes into your sleep-clouded mind. "Something's not right here, Raistlin! Come quick!"

His troubled tone startles you from your makeshift bed. Tossing aside your blanket, you hurriedly scramble to your feet. The sight that greets your still unfocused eyes jolts your brain to full wakefulness in an instant.

Not a hundred feet in front of your camp stands a very dark, dense, mist-draped forest—a forest that was not there last night!

A strange and powerful aura radiates from the forest. What seems to be a living essence reaches out to you from within its dark recesses. It touches your soul, and you shiver unconsciously. Swirling mists cling to the branches and boil around the roots of squat, twisted trees. Faint, wispy arms of fog strain like tethered creatures toward you from across the distance, only to be pulled back by some magical force. The pale light from the overcast early dawn sky doesn't even begin to penetrate the forest's shadowy darkness.

Caramon shakes his head in disbelief. From the look on his face, you know that he, too, senses the evil that lurks within those woods.

"Raistlin," he says quietly, as though trying to avoid being overheard, "you and I have suffered through a great deal to get here. We've seen and fought many strange things. But this forest has me at the end of my rope. If what you're looking for is beyond these woods, I'd like to know."

Resignedly you sink down onto a log. One of the hardest parts of the journey is now at hand—how to tell your twin brother what the future holds without telling him too much.

He respects the truth, you think quickly. *He may help me willingly if I give him some idea of what this place is. But if he finds out that these woods could well lead to our deaths, he will never let me go in. And above all else, I MUST GO IN!*

If you decide to tell Caramon a partial version of the truth, turn to **140**. If you think that you can bluff him into entering the woods with you, go to **164**.

95

Not only does the captain of the guard disappear, but the whole town also seems to melt into the ground. Whole chunks of buildings fall from their foundations and slip into the ground as though it were water. Soon nothing stands before you but a dirt road and a signpost pointing the way to Solace.

You look down the road toward your hometown with a warm, self-satisfied feeling inside. *He said I did well, and of course I did,* you think smugly. *Well, what else did they expect of me, anyway? Now let's go see what Solace has to offer.* You are almost whistling as you set foot on the road to your hometown. Add 1 point to your experience point total and turn to **27**.

96

Still the list of spells continues to eat at your mind. It must be good for something or it wouldn't have been put there. So what is it?

Suddenly it hits you. Of course! It's a list of the spells you'll need to face the fourth phase of your Test—Continual Light, Magic Missile, and Web! That must be it!

You stop a few minutes to look through your spellbook and gather the spells you want to take with you.

If you think the list is indeed a clue to the spells you need for the last trial, select them. If you think that it may be just a trick, choose any ones you want from section **10**—two first level spells and one second level spell. Be sure to record your spells on the back of your Character Stats Card.

Once you have selected your spells, you are prepared to enter the cavern beyond. Turn to **199**.

97

The haunting voice of the spectral minion bites straight into your heart.

"Young fool," he whispers harshly, "did you think that bluster could make up for your puny spells? Have you learned nothing? I am almost of a mind to send your corpse home this very instant. But that is not my mission. I was to test you and, if necessary, teach you a lesson. That I have done. But the lesson is not quite finished. Look upon me and see what the future holds for you should you continue on!" Turn to **145**.

98

You reach out with the magic of your Charm Person spell and penetrate the mind of the dragonman with the whip. The creature is weak and easy to control. At the same time, you jump from your hiding place.

"Help!" you shout. "These lizard creatures are after me! Please help!"

Startled, the other small dragonman spins to face you and pulls out its sword.

But the dragonman you charmed moves like lightning. Its sword already drawn, in a flash it buries the blade hilt deep into the back of its former companion.

At that moment, you witness an amazing thing. The body of the dying dragonman begins to stiffen before your eyes. Even as the dead creature falls to the floor, it grows rigid. When it hits the floor, it has turned to stone, locking the sword in its petrified body!

But, with or without its sword, the charmed dragonman is already on the attack. With a snarl of anger, it leaps across the room toward its former leader.

Snarling viciously, the leader flies to the attack itself. The dragonmen meet in midair and crash to the ground, locked in mortal combat. The charmed dragonman is the smaller of the two, and you can see it is getting the worst of things. You begin to prepare another spell to come to its aid, but at that moment, the gully dwarves, enraged at the beating of the female, pour out of the pot and attack the leader, too!

They swarm all over the struggling figures, biting and kicking at the larger dragonman. Pulling the mace from the creature's grasp, they pound it on its scaly head. Finally many pairs of small hands drag the two combatants to the edge of the hole. With a mighty heave, the dwarves toss them both through the hole! Then, whooping in triumph, the gully dwarves scurry off down one of the tunnels.

Suddenly you feel very strange. You look up to see the walls of the chamber beginning to shimmer with a strange, iridescent light, as if some powerful magic is at work! Turn to **123**.

99

You stand before the door bearing the white triangle. It appears to be made of solid gold, polished to a mirrorlike luster you can see yourself in. As you reach out to grab the handle of the door, you are startled to feel warmth radiating from it. Since it doesn't feel hot enough to burn you, you turn the handle and push.

Much to your surprise, the door swings open easily—so easily, in fact, that you stumble headlong into the next room.

Much to your amazement, you land on a dirt road! It isn't a room at all!

You rise to your feet and gape dumbly for a moment at the green, rolling hills and small groves of trees that greet your sight. The sun is shining and birds are singing. It seems to be a pleasant, summer day much like many others you've experienced in the country near your home in Solace. You turn around and see that the towers are still behind you, but the golden door is closed tight. When you test it, it won't open. It appears that you're here to stay—at least for a while.

You turn again to survey the land spreading out before you, puzzled by what you see. "Where have they sent me?" you say aloud. "This certainly isn't the Wayreth Forest that surrounds the towers. Where am I?"

The narrow road stretches out toward hills some distance in front of you. You can barely make out what seems to be a fork in the road—and a signpost! You hurry down the road toward the fork, hoping the sign will give you some idea as to where—and when!—you might be.

But the sign proves to be more of an enigma than a solution. One of the forks is labeled "TO SOLACE'S BULLIES" while the sign on the other fork reads "TO VERDIN'S CLERIC."

As you look down the road leading toward Solace, you can see in the distance a great stand of mighty vallenwood trees. Your home town of Solace is built within the great branches of such trees, and seeing them brings back memories. Can it be that you have returned home simply by walking through a door?

As you turn your head to look up the fork toward Verdin, you see that the road is soon lost among the rolling hills. Beyond the hills, the ground rises to a high plateau. Atop this plateau, surrounded by a wall, is a small castle. Flags fly from its parapets and its walls seem to be decorated with streamers of bright colors. *A festival of some kind, perhaps,* you think. *Well, I can find out soon enough. But why do that town and castle seem so familiar to me?*

Even as you stand puzzling over that, another thought troubles you. Since the Cataclysm, there have been no real clerics, those endowed by the gods with the power to heal, in Krynn. You yourself have searched with your friends for such power. To your dismay, all you found were false clerics, intent only upon swindling the people they supposedly were helping. *What is a cleric doing in my Test—if he is a cleric at all?* you wonder.

You realize you are getting nowhere as you stand here thinking. You're going to have to decide where to head first.

If you decide to go to Solace first, turn to **27**. If you'd rather go find out about the cleric at Verdin, turn to **2**.

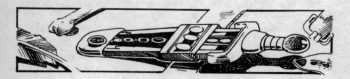

92

100

As the giant ogredog prepares to attack, you feel the excitement that combat always brings shoot through you. Trained reflexes respond to the threat as they have to so many others. Fighting is familiar to you and your brother, and you react like the finely honed fighting team you are.

Before the beast can make its initial charge, you leap from your horses. You land facing away from the ogredog, so that you can use your steeds as living walls to hide behind for a few precious seconds.

The monster hesitates, momentarily confused. Its prey has apparently disappeared. But that momentary pause is all the time you need.

Suddenly Caramon charges from behind his mount, bellowing a fierce war cry. The huge creature spins and begins to stalk toward him, howling a reply to his challenge.

The ogredog fails to realize its peril. While your brother dances before it, taunting and feinting in and out, you have time to cast your spell.

Turn to the Spell Resolution Table in section **10**. Follow the line that lists the spell you want to cast until you come to section **100**. Then turn to the section listed at the junction of the column and the row to discover the effect of the spell you selected.

101

"Idiotic riddles," you mutter. "If I'm supposed to go one way or the other, why can't they just tell me and be done with it?"

Since you can make neither heads nor tails of the poem, you are now faced with the option of going left or right.

If you decide to go left, go to **118**. If you choose to go to the right, go to **132**.

102

You know that your skill has met its ultimate test! The room is filling rapidly with an inky blackness. The drow, with its infravision, is sure to obliterate you in the darkness.

Quickly you pull what could be your salvation from your robe. If you can only read it before the darkness blocks out the light—and you!

Roll one die and add the result to your agility skill score. If the total is 10 or more, after adding any experience points you elect to use, turn to **115**. If it is less than 10, turn to **89**.

103

"Raistlin . . . Raistlin, wake up! Drink this. It'll give you strength."

Pain forms a warm, throbbing cocoon about you. Waking up only makes you more aware of the pain.

Through foggy eyes, you can see Caramon, blood-stained and weary, kneeling by your side. A fire burns behind him. Beyond that, the sun is setting, and the stars are beginning to appear in the light-washed sky.

Caramon lifts your head slowly to let you drink some of the soup he has heated. Its warmth flows down your throat and into the ache that is your shoulder. Then he eases your head back down onto your blanket roll.

"Well, little brother, that's over with. It was touch and go there for a while. I thought that beast had taken off your whole arm. As it is, he tore it up pretty badly. Broke your shoulder and collarbone. You've lost a lot of blood, too. You're going to have to rest here awhile before we head home."

Home! you think frantically. "But the Test!" you mutter weakly. "What about the Test?"

"Hang the Test!" he replies quickly. "You can't even stand up, let alone take any Test! We're getting out of here just as soon as you can travel. You'll have to face the Test another time."

Another time? you wonder. *Will there be another time?* It matters very little now. You know you couldn't stand up to the Test in this condition. Caramon is right. To rest now and then go home is what is important. After you are healed, you can return to try again.

If they'll let you.

104

The spectral minion stands in the gates of the towers, his arms crossed on his chest. You pull up your horse some distance from the hooded figure, and the air becomes strangely silent, as though the spectre was waiting for you to do something.

Fear rises within you, and you realize that you cannot face this fearsome creature again, especially if you must fight him to gain access inside the towers.

"Caramon," you whisper tersely, "we cannot enter here. I cannot face this being again. We'll have to seek another entrance."

Immediately the scene before you begins to change. The walls of the tower and the woods around you begin to fade. They seem to evaporate like so much mist.

Then a voice rings in the air, and you recognize it as the voice of Par-Salian himself, the master of mages! Turn to **210**.

105

This ought to teach that tyrant a lesson, you think. You blow grains of powdered brass from your palm and point your finger at the leader.

The magic force of your Push spell arcs its way across the room and slams into the lead dragonman.

One moment, the creature is watching its orders being carried out. The next, it is toppling into the hole, right into the pot with the gully dwarves.

The dwarves are quick to respond, beating, tearing, biting, and pounding their chief tormentor.

The dragonman's added weight causes the pot to begin to descend rapidly through the hole. In a moment, it disappears beneath the floor, and the screeches of pain from the dragonman and howls of glee from the dwarves fade into the distance.

The other two dragonmen move quickly to the edge of the hole, forgetting about their victim. As they stop and look down, you hear a shrieked command from far below, and they dive into the hole after the pot.

Suddenly you feel very strange. You look up to see the walls of the chamber beginning to shimmer with a strange, iridescent light, as if some powerful magic is at work! Turn to **123**.

106

What is the meaning of this attack? you think frantically. *There should be no obstacles to our passing. We are invited guests! This must be another part of the trial!*

Realization stuns you back to reality. You see Caramon standing now with sword upraised, responding in the only way he understands to the fear that assails him. But he must not strike the hooded figure!

"Caramon. Wait."

He hesitates momentarily. His whole body is intent on launching an attack on the robed being. Will he listen to you or ignore you and press his attack?

Roll one die and add the result to your presence skill score. If the total is 7 or more, turn to **55**. If it is less than 7, turn to **113**.

107

You blow the powdered brass you hold in your palm toward your opponent, and the invisible force from your Push spell slams into his legs. They're swept out from under him, and he drops to the ground face-first, striking his head on a rock. He shakes his head and struggles to rise for a moment, then slumps, unconscious, to the ground.

Half expecting the rest of the bullies to flee, you look up just in time to see a club flying at you. It catches you squarely in the ribs, and you feel one of them snap. More blows begin to rain upon you, pummeling you into a senseless stupor. The right-hand man steps into view and swings his club one last time. It slams into your forehead, and everything goes black.

Subtract 3 points from your hit point total and turn to **219**.

108

You carefully consider what you may be facing. Fistandantalus had said it would be very difficult.

He also said you'd be free to use any of your spells. *He'd better mean they'll be there in my mind when I need them,* you think. *I haven't had a chance to study them. But what am I up against, anyway—some new monster? A magic-user?* Your mind recalls the wizard's workroom and the overturned bottles and disturbed equipment. It could well be that some other spellcaster is in here with you, facing his own test!

As you recall details about the workroom, you remember something else. Of course! The list! The treasure at the end of the second phase was a scroll with a list of spells on it. What had it said? Yes, you remember it quite clearly: "Continual Light, Magic Missile, Web, Staff."

But what is this combination of spells good for? Could that list have some bearing on what you are about to face?

If you received the Staff of Magius, turn to **35**. If you received the Continual Light spell scroll, go to **135**. If you have neither the staff or the scroll, turn to **50**.

109

Despite the almost overwhelming fear gnawing at you, your brain is still able to function with cold, hard reason. *Of course, you idiot!* you think. *These feelings of fear and these otherworldly voices are nothing more than part of the protective spell that blocks passage through the wood from all but the most determined. Mere voices can do us no harm!* And with that understanding comes calmness.

"Do not be afraid, Caramon," you say aloud, overcoming your own clouded thinking. "These feelings of fear are all part of the magical barrier. Pay them no heed and they will vanish like the dew. As for the way into the forest, it will be provided."

"Look, Raist," your brother says, not sounding very reassured by your advice, "let's just go home. Whatever is in there doesn't want us in there with it, and I . . . I . . ."

His words trail off as his jaw drops open. In wide-eyed disbelief, he stammers, "R-R-Raistlin, look at the forest! It's moving!"

You spin about, facing the forest. You half expect to see some monstrous beast springing at you from the mists. What greets your eyes instead is enough to drive a sane person mad.

The forest itself is opening up in front of your horse!

Turn to **216**.

The surging crowd sweeps you with it into the town square. Once inside, you fight your way to one side to get a better view of whatever is about to happen.

In the center of the square, a platform has been erected. On the platform is an altar of sorts, and beside the altar sits a small pile of wood. The scene has all the earmarks of some sort of . . .

Sacrifice? you think with a start. *Does this cleric intend to make a sacrifice to his new gods?*

A hush falls over the crowd as the cleric Verminaard moves to the altar and throws back the hood of his simple black robe to reveal his face. It fairly beams with benevolence and honesty, but as he casts his gaze slowly over the crowd, you catch a glimmer in his eyes that reminds you somehow of a snake. You are convinced that this man is up to no good!

As the cleric raises his hands, the crowd grows silent. In a voice as rich and smooth as oil, Verminaard begins to speak.

"I bring you hope for a new tomorrow in the name of the new gods!" he cries.

The crowd erupts in cheers and applause. After a few seconds, the cleric silences them and continues. You listen with growing distaste as he starts to berate the old gods who served Krynn for eons, deriding them for forsaking Krynn in its time of need. It was the fault of the old gods, he says, not the false pride of the people, that brought the Cataclysm and poverty and death. It was time for the world to turn to gods who would succor them in their time of trial. It was time for the new gods.

Verminaard's voice fills the air with promises of better

times ahead, all in the name of the new gods. The crowd listens, spellbound, hanging on every word he says.

Make a reasoning check at this point. Roll one die and add the result to your reasoning skill score. If the total is 6 or more, turn to **32**. If it is less than 6, go to **59**.

111

As tiny grains of sand trickle from your hand, you murmur, *"Ast tasarak simiralan krynawi."*

Your spell silently gathers the magic forces of Sleep to do your bidding. Your mind sends the spell to engulf the two smaller dragonmen.

The whip in the creature's clawed hand wavers. In a second, the whip falls to the floor, followed by the two dragonmen. With a crash, they slump down in a deep slumber.

For a moment, there is silence. Then chaos breaks loose.

The leader roars a command and strides across the room toward its fallen subordinates. "Get up, you louts!" it shouts. "We have no time for jokes!"

The dwarves, on the other hand, go wild. The lead dragonman has moved well away from them, and the other two are sprawled on the floor. The dwarves scramble out of the pot, whooping and hollering, and scurry off down the other tunnel.

The remaining dragonman looks about suspiciously. Cursing the dwarves and its sleeping comrades, it turns and heads for the hole in the floor. It stops at the edge and rummages for something in a small pouch hanging from its belt. Then it pulls out a small object that you cannot see very clearly. Muttering under its breath, it steps into the hole and disappears from sight.

Make a check of your reasoning skill. Roll one die and add the result to your reasoning skill score. If the total is 7 or more, turn to **146**. If it is less than 7, go to **37**.

112

Fortunately the troubling thoughts that bothered you as you fell asleep don't hinder your rest. You sleep soundly and awake refreshed, ready to memorize your spells for the next phase of the Test.

Refer to section **10** as much as you need to, then write the three spells you choose to take on the third phase of your Test on the back of your Character Stats Card. You may select two first level spells and one second level spell. Keep in mind the spell components you have already selected.

After some time, you come out of your trancelike memorization state, your spells firmly in mind. Rising to your feet, you turn and leave the room by the small door next to the shelves.

Once more you find yourself in the familiar corridor, facing the last door in your Test—the future. Who knows what the future will hold in store for you? There is only one way to find out. With a firm resolve to succeed or to die trying, you reach out and turn the handle of the steel door with the black triangle on it.

Turn to **43**.

113

Caramon sees only the danger before him and continues to advance threateningly. "Stay, minion!" he bellows loudly. "You face your death if you molest us further!"

The figure halts momentarily, looking toward you as if expecting something. When you do nothing, it merely shrugs and advances again.

Caramon charges forward, bringing his sword down in a slashing arc. At the last moment, he feints to his right, and his downswing becomes a vicious backhand slash across his opponent's neck.

But the blow never lands!

You gape in amazement. As the blade touches the hooded figure, he instantly "blinks" a yard or so behind where he was standing, and Caramon's sword whistles harmlessly through thin air.

The powerful stroke spins the young warrior completely around, and he tumbles to the ground in a heap.

Quickly he recovers and springs to his feet. He begins to circle to one side.

Curiously, the spectral being stops moving and turns slowly to face your brother. Opening its arms wide, it seems to invite an attack.

Enraged, Caramon wastes no time and slams a savage thrust into the creature's belly.

The inevitable happens. A deep-throated roar of pain echoes through the mists. You watch Caramon double over and fall. His sword arm, charred black and twisted in pain, is clutched desperately to his stomach as he writhes in agony on the ground. Smoke rises from the wounded arm as though it were burning. Caramon stares up at the minion in helpless, abject fear, powerless to do anything.

The creature seems not to notice him. It slowly pulls the smoking blade from its midsection and tosses it aside disdainfully, then stands over Caramon with hand upraised.

If you want to go to your brother's aid, turn to **41**. If you decide to wait for the spectral minion to come to you, go to **175**. If you elect to cast a magic spell at the spectre, turn to **119**.

114

As you begin to move into the almost tomblike stillness of your hometown, you are startled by a peal of raucous laughter, followed by a loud shout.

Another sound of unpleasant laughter spins you around. To your surprise, you find yourself facing a young man on the road some ten feet behind you. He has a swarthy look to him and seems to be a few years younger than you—perhaps sixteen or seventeen. He looks vaguely familiar.

"Well, what a pleasant surprise," he sneers, eyeing you evilly. "Look who's here . . . and without his big lout of a brother around, either. How nice of you to come visit us, *magician.*"

He practically spits the last word from his mouth, as if it tastes bad. Then he looks around at the silent town and shouts, "Hey, fellas, gather 'round! Look what I've found!"

Slowly, from behind trees and carts, several other youths appear. They form a large circle around you. You notice that two of them are hefting nasty-looking clubs.

The first youth, obviously their leader, snorts, "You made me look like a fool once, trickster—right in front of everyone. Well, now you'll pay for that!"

Your memory focuses sharply on his words, and suddenly

you remember. In your younger days, you had indeed humiliated this youngster at a public gathering after he and his companions had tormented you mercilessly. He and his friends would have trounced you then and there had your brother Caramon not intervened. But now there is no Caramon here, and they seem intent on getting their revenge.

Roll one die and add the result to your presence skill score. Remember to subtract 1 from your die roll if you saw the face of the spectral minion in the Wayreth Forest. If the total is 6 or more, turn to **168**. If it is less than 6, go to **207**.

115

Gilean be praised! You're blessed with an almost godlike speed. Before the drow can complete its spell, you have your Continual Light scroll in hand. Arcane words spill from your mouth in a matter of seconds.

A small sun explodes inside the cavern, dazzling your eyes.

Your opponent screeches in anger and pain, blinded by the blazing light. The drow throws its hands up in front of its eyes and turns away from the piercing light.

You have bought yourself valuable time, but you must hurry. The drow isn't going to succumb that easily. Unless you miss your guess, it will rebound fast. As if in answer to your thoughts, the drow stands and turns to the fray again.

Roll one die and add the result to your agility skill score. If the total is 9 or more, turn to **10** and select your spell. If it is less than 9, go to **3**.

116

Your spell has absolutely no effect on the beast. You watch helplessly as Caramon tries to fight the monster on his own.

If you want to try to cast another spell, turn to section **10** and try again. If you end up here once more, turn to **205**.

If you elect not to use any more magic, roll one die and add the result to your reasoning skill score. If the total is 6 or more, turn to **84**. If it is less than 6, turn to **205**.

When you come to, you are lying on the floor of the corridor. Your robes are still smoldering from the fire, but at least you're not burned to a crisp. As you rise painfully to your feet, a dusty voice speaks softly inside your mind.

"Foolish boy, will you never learn? I am not in the habit of giving assistance only to have it cast aside. Consider again my message. And this time, do not be so foolhardy."

Subtract 3 points from your hit point total, then return to **125** and choose again.

118

You soon find that the left-hand tunnel is none too smooth and is full of dank, dead air. The light globes are farther apart now, making this tunnel almost murky. The tunnel bears steadily to the left, forming what seems to be a circle.

You advance carefully. You may yet be able to surprise whatever may be lurking in the tunnel. Your stomach is full of butterflies and your body is tense as you sneak along.

You round a bend and find yourself facing a solid brick wall. No other corridor branches off to either side, and you know you haven't passed any. You realize you'll have to take the other corridor.

Turn to **132**.

119

Something inside you snaps! You step forward in an unmistakable challenge.

"Foul villain!" you thunder. "How dare you hinder the passage of your betters? Stand aside, or taste the wrath of him whose pardon you will beg when he has finished with you!"

Your opponent stops, gauging your challenge. "Young pup," he intones, "you have a great deal to learn. I look for-

105

ward to giving you your first lesson. We shall see who grovels at whose feet when all is said and done. Proceed, insignificant trickster!"

His words sting you once more. Your rage flares to a peak as you decide your course of action.

To choose the spell you wish to use against your antagonist, turn to section **10** and locate the section to turn to as you have done previously by cross-indexing the name of the spell you wish to cast with the number of this section.

If you have no spells left to cast, go to **195**.

120

A curtain of darkness descends around you as Fistandantalus's great hall disappears. In a few moments, the curtain rises again, revealing a dimly lit, irregular tunnel. It's fairly wide and paved with stone. Every ten feet or so, you see a torch in a wall sconce, providing enough light to see by. There's a solid wall behind you, leaving only one way to go.

"Well, at least I don't have to choose which way to go," you say softly to the air.

You pad along the winding tunnel as cautiously and quietly as your booted feet will allow. After perhaps forty feet, the tunnel turns sharply to the right. Slowly you peer around the corner into what appears to be a large chamber.

Whatever awaits me must be here, you think. *Collect your wits, my friend, and prepare to face the inevitable.*

Roll one die and add the result to your reasoning skill score. If the total is 7 or more, turn to **108**. If it is less than 7, go to **144**.

121

Even as the arcane words of the spell pass from your lips, you realize your mistake. You need a material component for this spell!

Caramon launches his muscular body across the space separating the two of you. You rummage frantically through your robe. If you can only find the right component in time. . . .

Turn to **177**.

Hunched over the little female gully dwarf is something resembling a man. It's man-sized and walks on two bent legs, but it's covered with thin scales and has a flat reptilian head that ends in a sharp, toothy snout. Its hands and feet end in cruel-looking claws, and from its back extend a pair of batlike, leathery wings.

If anyone had ever conceived of combining the seed of man with that of dragonkind, this might have been the result. You can barely contain a gasp of astonishment at first sight of this terrible dragonman.

As your eyes sweep the room, you notice that there are three of the strange creatures in the room. One stands next to the first, hissing a cruel laugh at the female gully dwarf's torment. The other, bigger and more heavily armed than the first two, is stationed next to the pot. It holds a wicked-looking steel mace and carries itself with an air of authority. You guess it must be their leader.

The dragonman with the whip looms over the helpless gully dwarf, raises the whip, and hisses, "Get up, you filthy scum, and climb into the pot, or I'll flay the meat from your bones!"

The little gully dwarf, on her knees before the creature, straightens up and shrieks defiantly, "No! No go down work. No more work for spawn lizard bosses. You all drop dead. May Great Lizard chew your bones and trample your heads!"

You watch as the lash comes down again. The gully dwarf cries out in pain and falls face forward to the stone floor.

The other dragonman near her kicks her savagely in the ribs, and a low groan escapes from the prostrate body. It's answered by a loud moan of sympathy from the pot of gully dwarves. The one who seems to be the leader of the dragonmen strikes the pot with its mace. "Silence, dwarf swine!" it hisses loudly. "Now do you see the reward for disobeying orders?"

The scaly creature raises its whip again, and the little gully dwarf kneels up resolutely, death written on her face.

You can't stand by any longer and watch these evil creatures beat a helpless gully dwarf!

Two possible courses of action pass through your mind. You could attack the leader magically, perhaps disheartening the other dragonmen, or you can cast a spell on the smaller dragonmen and deal with the larger creature later.

If you wish to attack the leader with a spell, turn to **202**. If you decide to attack the smaller two first, turn to **20**.

123

When the effects of the magic finally disappear, you find yourself standing in the middle of a great hall. It's dark, except for a single shaft of light from some unseen source high above you. It casts a large pool of light on the floor at the far end of the hall.

In the center of the light sits a throne, and on the throne sits a man heavily shrouded in black robes. His face is hidden within the folds of his hood.

"Well, youngster," says the figure, "step closer so we can talk." The voice is dusty, full of whispering sand, and seems to echo hollowly down a long tunnel. It is very soft but penetrates your hearing and every part of your mind.

You remember this voice from earlier in the Test. Your unknown benefactor has made his appearance at last!

You cross the stone floor obediently. As you step into the light, the rest of your surroundings disappear from sight. You are alone with this being.

"You have done reasonably well, Raistlin," your host continues. "You have survived all three phases of your trial. You are to be congratulated. You seem to be all that the Shapers of the Test had hoped—and more. But the entire truth of that remains to be seen.

"You stand now in a realm outside the plane of the Test. I doubt that Par-Salian is aware of your absence. That matters little, really, since there is nothing he can do about it. For the moment, you must be here.

"Know I am one of the Shapers of your Test—in fact, its prime Shaper. It was I you faced in the Wayreth Forest, and again at the gates of the towers. It was I who provided clues and spells to you during the Test. I, above all, am responsible for your being here, because I need you! I am Fistandantilus, and you must now stand in judgment before me!"

Turn to **163**.

124

"Caramon, keep your blade sheathed and stand aside!" you command icily. "I will see to this."

He whirls on you. Terror and rage fill his eyes.

"No, Raistlin," he says thickly, "*you* be still! I've had enough of this place and your bossing. I'll deal with this lowlife in a manner most befitting to his station, and you will not hinder me!"

The tension he has been under since early this morning has taken control of him. Nothing you can do or say can hold him now, and you know it. He pulls out his sword and whirls to face the hooded figure. Turn to **113**.

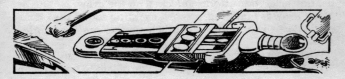

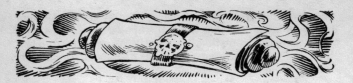

125

Pondering the meaning of the strange message, you gaze thoughtfully at the doors before you. Each is marked with a symbol. When you examine them more closely, you find that the symbol on each door is a simple triangle. The door directly in front of you bears a red triangle, the door to your left carries a black triangle, and the door to your right bears a white triangle.

What can all this mean? you think. *What do the past, present, and future have to do with my Test? And how am I to know which of these doors leads to which point in time? Could there be some clue in the message my mysterious benefactor left behind? On the other hand, perhaps it doesn't really matter at all where I start. . . .*

All these thoughts fill in your head as you try to decide what to do.

If you think you should try to figure out which of the doors leads to the past, present, and future, then face the tests in that order, turn to **154**. But if you simply want to begin by passing through one of the three doors regardless of any order, turn to **192**.

126

As quickly as possible, you mutter the words of your Invisibility spell. *The drow can't hit what it can't see,* you think hopefully.

You feel the magic mantle drape over you and, reassured by your invisibility, start to move into position for your next attack, your attention locked on the drow.

The drow is laughing, a short, cackling sound that sends chills down your spine. Then it begins to mutter another spell.

With unerring certainty, the drow looks right at you! "Ah, trickster," it cackles, "how rude of you to try to disappear before we've finished our little business with each other." With a sinking feeling, you realize it has cast a Detect Invisibility spell. Turn to **3**.

"... *tobanis kar!*"

Two brightly glowing white darts spring to the tips of your fingers. Then, instantly, they streak through the air toward your brother. He has no time to dodge, nor could he even if there were time. A magic missile never misses.

The fiery missiles slam into Caramon with awesome force. One catches him squarely in the center of his armored chest, and the other lances into his right shoulder. You watch as he is literally knocked off his feet, crashing to the ground in a tangle of flesh and armor.

You stand beside your horse, berating yourself at having had to use such a powerful force against your own brother. He was only acting in what he thought to be your best interest.

"Caramon," you say remorsefully, "I *must* go into that forest. It is the most important thing I have yet done in my life. Can you understand that now?"

You watch as your twin raises himself up on one elbow. He is wounded, but his eyes show that physical pain is not what has hurt him the most. He stares at you for a few seconds and shakes his head, obviously unable to believe that you, of all people, would attack him. You see that he is breathing hard from the pain, and he has to tighten his jaw to gain control before he can speak. Turn to **58**.

128

The words of your Web spell spring to your lips. As they do, the tiny strand of spiderweb floats from your fingertips and lands unseen at the feet of the lead dragonman.

Immediately it starts to grow. Sticky tendrils of webbing sprout up from the floor at the creature's feet. More spill down from the ceiling to entangle it from above. Soon it is completely covered in sticky webbing.

But to your surprise, the dragonman leader tears the webbing from its body as if it were paper. Roaring a command, it points its mace in your direction. By some incredible sixth sense, it has followed the trail of your spell. It glares knowingly into your hiding place.

The two smaller dragonmen turn toward you. They draw their swords and prepare to charge. Perhaps you can cast another spell at them before they get to you if you hurry! Turn to **167**.

129

As fast as the drow is, you move even faster! As the darkness threatens to entomb you, you summon your Continual Light spell from the Staff of Magius.

"*Shirak!*" you shout feverishly.

The ball at the end of the staff bursts into a miniature sun. Blazing, blinding light fills the cavern, and the drow screeches in pain and hides its head behind its cape.

You have gained a slight advantage. Though the drow is hurt, you know the light will not stop it for long. You must make your next spell count before it can turn on you.

Almost in answer to your fears, the drow straightens and turns to face you once more.

Roll one die and add the result to your agility skill score. If the total is 9, including whatever experience points you may choose to spend, go to **10** and select your next spell. If it is less than 9, turn to **3**.

130

The fear that has threatened to dominate your actions rises now to new intensity, crushing your confidence.

"No," you whisper, "I will not—I cannot—proceed."

Par-Salian rises slowly to his feet. It is as though your decision has added an extra burden to his already weighty responsibility. "So be it, young mage. This is where it will end. Know that we had high hopes for you. Now only the future will tell what is in store for you—and the rest of us."

The ancient mage raises his hands skyward and begins to mutter the words of a powerful incantation, one you have never heard before and may never hear again. To your amazement, everything around you begins to disappear.

The towers, the forest, the mist—everything fades to nothing. Soon all that remains is a grassy valley floor that stretches out before you, the wind whispering softly through the grass as it passes.

Suddenly Par-Salian's voice speaks from the air around you. Turn to **210**.

131

You stand in the road at the edge of town and ponder the events of the first two trials. Your thoughts are dark as you wait for something to "happen along."

I hope the Shapers of the Test don't expect me to face such elementary tests as the ones so far. What am I to learn from those experiences that will make me a great magician? And how long must I wait here—and for what?

Your thoughts are interrupted by a distant rumbling sound. As you listen, it becomes steadily louder until you recognize hoofbeats. It sounds like a whole herd of hoofed beasts approaching you!

But you sense that something is wrong. The ground should be trembling from the weight of so many large animals approaching. Instead, the ground is still. It is the air that is reverberating around you!

Suddenly you see a moving sparkle in the sky. You look up, and your heart almost stops beating. For there, galloping down from a bank of clouds, is a sight that few on Krynn can ever hope to see.

The creature's dark golden mane and beard flow back over its luminescent golden body. A single twisted horn extends from its forehead, and its golden-pink hooves sparkle with a brilliance that rivals the stars. The air at its feet seems to be on fire as it thunders through the sky. You realize that you are the center of attention of a legendary Kirin. Turn to **48**.

132

The right-hand tunnel is fairly smooth. Its floor, however, is not made of stone but soft, warm sand. More of the strange light globes fill the tunnel with a soft glow, making it feel almost homey here.

It's best not to let myself get too comfortable, you think. *There's no telling what might lie beyond the bend ahead.*

The tunnel bears steadily to your right, forming part of what seems to be a circle. You advance carefully, hoping that you may yet be able to surprise whatever may be lurking down here. Your body is tense as you sneak along.

You've moved only thirty feet or so into the tunnel when an ear-shattering roar fills the passageway, shaking the very walls. Your heart leaps to your throat, and you slam yourself against the wall to hide from sight. The roar comes again, a tortured, almost heart-rending howl that gradually changes to vengeful, unbridled rage.

Whatever's down there isn't in any mood to receive visitors, you think.

You have an urge to turn back, but you remember Par-Salian's warning about running away from any part of your Test. And it's entirely possible that whatever creature is lurking down there could attack you from behind the second you turned your back to go the other way.

You have no choice except to go on. Turn to **24**.

133

". . . kairtangus miopiar!"

A fan-shaped shower of flames leaps from the outstretched fingers of your joined hands. You feel the intense heat of the flames wash across your face.

Before Caramon can move, the fan of flames strikes him full in the chest. Instinctively he throw his arms over his face and turns away. The flames spray across his back and singe his hair as a howl of pain escapes from his throat. He

115

doubles over and falls to his knees on the ground.

Your hands drop to your side and the spell fades. Immediately chagrined at having injured your brother, you hurry to his side to try to comfort him. His tunic and hair are still smoldering, but he's not burned nearly as badly as you feared. His armor has protected him from the worst of the damage. As he turns to face you, hurt fills his eyes.

"I'm sorry, Caramon," you begin lamely, "but you tried to hinder me in the most important event of my life. Now can you see that I must go into the forest—at any cost?"

Your brother looks up at you. Tears of pain and hurt well up in his eyes, tearing at your heart. Then he tightens his jaw to gain some control before he speaks. Turn to **58.**

134
You stifle a scream as the speeding Ki-rin hits the castle wall. Incredibly, you feel no sensation of crashing into a wall. All sensation of movement simply ceases.

You drop your arms from in front of your face and slowly open your eyes. You are still mounted on the Ki-rin's back, but you are both standing in a room the likes of which you have never seen before!

You slide off your fabulous mount and walk over to examine the wall nearest you. Your eyes fall on several sets of shelves containing an assortment of bottles and vials filled with what must be magic components. There is also a large table beneath the shelving. Scattered on top of it, you see various tools and instruments of magical experimentation. You have never seen a mage's workroom so well stocked with useful—and terrible—items.

The sight of such wondrous magical elements within your reach reminds you of your own spell components. Almost absentmindedly, your hand begins to probe the hidden pockets and pouches of your robe, checking to make sure that all is in order. But as you search each pocket, you begin to panic. You grab frantically at your robe, almost ripping it in two. All your spell components have vanished! Turn to **65**.

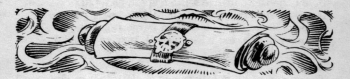

135

You have a Continual Light spell on the scroll, but what is this staff referred to on the list? You seem to be only half-prepared.

But, you recall, Fistandantalus said, "Together we can conquer anything."

I hope he meant this, too, you think.

Roll one die and add the result to your reasoning skill score. If the total is 9 or more, turn to **96**. If it is less than 9, choose three spells from your spellbook in section **10**—two first level spells and one second level spell—and turn to **199**.

136

As the bullies continue to advance, your mind reels. *If I can just get their leader out of the way, the rest may flee,* you think desperately.

You turn to face the leader of the group. "All right, you," you shout challengingly. "If you have a quarrel with me, let's settle it between the two of us—unless, of course, you haven't the courage to face me man-to-man!"

The leader's henchmen stop in their tracks as they look to their head man. He is obviously piqued by your words and can't afford to lose face in front of his followers.

"All right, then," he answers slowly. "So be it!" He turns to his right-hand man and whispers something. Then he approaches you cautiously.

As he circles, you close your eyes and begin to softly mutter a spell. When you open your eyes, he has closed within range. You slowly raise your hands and let loose your magic!

If you decide to use Burning Hands, turn to **176**.

If you choose to utilize a Push spell, go to **107**.

If you elect to throw a Magic Missile spell, turn to **56**.

If you want to throw a Charm Person spell, go to **63**.

If you prefer to cast a Sleep spell, turn to **148**.

137

The vision of your future has shaken you to your very roots. You cannot face the Test now. Now that you have seen your fate, you realize that it is too terrifying, the price too great.

As though reading your thoughts, the spectre speaks. His voice sounds almost disappointed.

"So be it, then. Let it end here. The supplicant is released from his quest."

Without warning, he vanishes into the mist. To your amazement, so does the forest. It seems to evaporate like dew before the morning sun. Soon all that is left is a grassy valley floor that stretches out before you. The wind whispers softly through the grass as it passes.

A voice speaks from the air around you. You recognize it as that of Par-Salian, the Master. Turn to **210**.

138

Hunched over the little female gully dwarf is something resembling a scaly man. It's man-sized and walks on bent legs, but it's covered from head to foot with thin scales that ripple over well-muscled legs and arms, and it wears a harness of chain mail. Its flat, reptilian head ends in a sharp, toothy snout, its hands and feet in cruel-looking claws. From its upper back extend a pair of batlike, leathery wings.

If anyone had ever conceived of combining the seed of man with that of dragonkind, this might have been the result.

As your eyes sweep the room, you notice three of the strange creatures. Two somewhat smaller dragonmen are standing over the gully dwarf, hissing cruel laughter at her torment. The third, bigger and better equipped than the first two, stands next to the pot. It holds a wicked-looking steel mace and carries itself with an air of authority. You guess it is their leader.

You can't stifle a gasp of astonishment at the sight of the terrible creatures. The gasp doesn't go unnoticed. The larger dragonman looks around the chamber, wondering where the noise came from. You know that you're going to have to act fast!

Roll one die. Since these things are new to you and rather formidable-looking, subtract 1 from the result and add the remainder to your agility skill score. If the total is 6 or more, turn to **20**. If it is less than 6, go to **167**.

139

The floor continues to rise slowly toward the ceiling as you kneel, searching frantically for something that might save you from certain death.

In the midst of your frenzied search, you hear another loud snapping sound. It's answered by a low whirring noise from somewhere above your head. You look up to see the ceiling beginning to move!

Before your startled, grateful eyes, the ceiling begins to slide to the side, revealing a large circular opening. As you rise through the ceiling, you breathe a sigh of relief.

You find yourself in familiar surroundings. Rows of shelves filled with small bottles greet your eyes. Familiar tables littered with equipment sit in the middle of the room. The smell of food reaches you from a small, low table to one side of the room.

You have returned to the wizard's workshop!

Turn to **6**.

140

"Very well, Caramon," you begin. "Since you already know that I seek the supreme test of my skills, you might as well know the rest." *At least* some *of the rest,* you add silently.

Your twin sits on a nearby log, eyeing you curiously as you continue.

"The end of our journey is far closer than you may think. Somehow we find ourselves standing before the Wayreth Forest, the last barrier between us and the fabled Towers of High Sorcery. It is the towers that are our destination. They are said to lie somewhere within this mystic wood, protected from prying eyes and unwelcome guests by ancient and horrible guardians. It is within the towers that I will face the Test, an ordeal that certain members of my order must endure to prove themselves. When I am finished with that ordeal, I will be a magician with powers the likes of which you have never seen!" *And your equal . . . or better,* you add silently.

Caramon's face pales slightly at the mention of the Towers of High Sorcery, the last stronghold of the most powerful and fearful magic-users on the world of Krynn. He has heard of the "black towers of arcane and unspeakable death," if only in whispered rumor. You turn and cast a dubious glance at the forest as you continue.

"Things have not happened as I foresaw, however. It seems that our destination has come to us. To tell the truth, this is not at all what I expected."

Your twin stares at you dumbly for a moment before he can speak. "You mean you knew this was where we were headed all along?" he asks.

"To an extent, yes," you counter, hedging a little as you continue to gaze into the dark wood. "I have been told that this forest can be found only by those invited to seek it. Apparently the opposite is more to the point. I was invited,

120

and the forest found me!"

"Invited?" the giant warrior questions. "What do you mean, 'invited' . . . and by whom?"

"I suppose you should know that, too," you reply. "About four months ago, Par-Salian, the greatest of my kind now living, appeared at our school of magic and asked me if I was ready to take the Test. Despite the protests of my headmaster, I advised Par-Salian that I was ready at any time.

" 'Prepare to leave in three months' time, then,' the ancient mage told me. 'Be sure to arrive when the Warrior and the Queen of Darkness first meet in nightly battle. Then we shall see what we shall see.'

"And so we are here," you conclude. "The wood lies before us, and the towers lie within the forest. You may come or stay behind, as you wish, my brother, but I *must* continue! What is your choice?"

Caramon stares at the ground for some time after you finish. You are not at all sure how he has taken your tale or what his reaction will be. But when he raises his head, somehow you know what he will say. Turn to **151**.

141

Through closed eyelids, you sense a bright light. The cold of the darkness is replaced by the comforting solidity of warm stone beneath your back. Slowly you open your eyes to discover yourself lying in the middle of an intersection in what appears to be a stone building or castle. Short passages, again lit by small globes, lead off in three directions. Each ends at a door.

As you rise slowly to your feet, the dusty, disembodied voice fills your head once more.

"Well, well, young apprentice," it chortles, "excellently done. Continue in this manner and you may yet succeed. But now I must leave you for a while. You will be on your own for the remainder of the Test, except for the message I shall leave behind. However, we may still meet again, if fate so dictates. And you may yet come to know who I am and exactly what I seek. Farewell!"

With a soft chuckle, the voice slowly fades from your hearing.

You turn back toward the three corridors, only to see a large stone slab lying on the floor of the corridor. It has some writing on it. *The message the voice said it would leave behind!* you think excitedly and begin to read it eagerly.

> Young mage, you should advised be,
> You'll face your Test through these doors three.
> The past through one—times you were shriven;
> Cleansed you may be, pure-white, forgiven.
> The present, too, has a door hidden here.
> Blood-red death, ever present, you must fear.
> Most terrible is door three, the future place,
> Beyond which you'll encounter a terrible face.
> A fourth trial, then, will be your lot.
> Without my help, you'll survive it not.
> But help I can, from unknown quarter;
> Be wise. Trust me. We need no martyr!
> Great magic of old can be my gift,
> An ancient staff which you can lift.
> And what will you give to me in return?
> A simple boon you will not spurn.

Turn to **125**.

142

"Well," you mutter, "that takes care of that. Now let's see what awaits me down that other tunnel!"

You cross the ogre mage's former prison chamber and enter the tunnel on the opposite side. After only a few feet, the tunnel opens into a circular stone room. Rising from the floor in the center of the room is a dais supporting a small altar. Resting on top of the altar lies a scroll.

"Is this all that's here?" you mutter in disappointment. "A simple scroll? What about the treasure the ogre mage spoke of?"

Despite your disappointment, your curiosity gets the best of you, and you carefully lift the scroll and open it. Written in glowing script is another message:

"Greetings! You have done well to have made it this far. Here is your reward. Remember these, for they will be important to your future:

"Continual Light
"Magic Missile
"Web
"Staff

"Use them wisely at the proper moment and you will succeed!"

As you finish reading the scroll, the words vanish from the page. Pondering their meaning, you tuck the scroll into your robes and start looking for an exit from the chamber. Turn to **93**.

143

The hollow voice of the spectral minion who assailed you reverberates from Caramon's mouth.

"The Shapers of the Test have been mistaken. They invited a witless dunce, a coward who surely would never have lived through the ordeal of the Test. It has therefore been decided that you must return to your home. Only time will tell if you ever get another chance to face the Test. But for now, you are to leave!"

The voice ceases and Caramon's eyes refocus. Nervously looking about, your brother rises to his feet, visibly shaken, and speaks to you in his own voice.

"What'd I tell you, Raistlin? Can't trust these mages, I said, huh? Wasn't I right? Come on, little brother. Let's go home."

You offer no protest as he helps you into your saddle. You are defeated. The spectral minion's message has sapped your last reserves. How cruel to send those words through Caramon! It seems you will never escape your twin's shadow. Misery devours you as you ride through the mists, away from the Towers of High Sorcery. Your chance to become one of Krynn's greatest wizards has come to an end.

144

You pause before entering the cavern to consider what you may be up against. Some new monster, perhaps, or maybe a magic-user like yourself.

"But what is there to consider?" you mumble. "I have my spells and my components. Fistandantalus said I would be free to use them. I hope that means the spells will come to me as bidden, since I haven't had a chance to memorize them."

You take a few minutes to sort through the spells in your spellbook and select the ones you wish to take into the cavern with you.

Choose two first level spells and one second level spell from section 10 and record them on the back of your Character Stats Card.

That done, you sit and reflect on your progress so far. *Why am I dawdling?* you think impatiently. *Let's just get this over with!*

Straightening your back, you walk resolutely around the corner into the cavern beyond. Turn to 199.

145

Slowly you raise your eyes to the hooded figure's head as he reaches up and pulls the hood back from his face. The sight makes you gasp.

The face is as gaunt as that of a man whose health has been sapped from him for years. A wracking cough shakes the figure before you, causing blood to trickle from his lips.

His skin is of an odd golden hue, almost metallic, while his hair is as white as snow.

But it is his eyes that frighten you most. Their pupils are shaped like hourglasses, and in them you see only death.

With a choking whisper, the ghastly visage continues. "Behold, and know that what you now see in me is what will be left of you when you complete the Test, if you survive the Test at all. Your health—even your very life force— will be sapped from you, leaving only what you see here. But I tell you also that the rewards of this fate, and the power it will lead to, are even greater than the price you must pay.

"I am empowered to offer you a choice," he continues. "You may go to the towers to face the Test and your future, or you may go home, unscathed except for this lesson. Should you leave, I cannot say whether you will ever come here again. Be warned, though, that if you proceed to the towers, you will face the Test at a considerable disadvantage."

He ceases to speak and waits for your decision. One of the

most difficult choices of your life is now before you. You have seen what could become of you. Are the rewards worth the sacrifice?

If you decide you are strong enough to face the Test and wish to continue, go to **79**. If, however, you would rather return to Solace and wait for another opportunity to face the Test, turn to **137**.

146

With the dragonmen gone, you cautiously leave your hiding place in the tunnel and head toward the prone gully dwarf. You keep a constant eye on the hole in the floor, though, in case any dragonmen appear. You want to be ready for them.

Something about the way the leader of the dragonmen left bothers you, though. In a flash, your mind reviews the last several seconds before it disappeared from the room. You remember that it pulled a small object out of its pouch and muttered some words over it. *Odd,* you think, *it looked very much like it was* casting a spell!

That's got to be it! you think desperately. *The dragonman didn't just drop into the hole, it actually disappeared from sight! It's become invisible!*

Panic grips you and you start to whirl about, looking for some sign of the dragonman, but your reason immediately turns you away from that course. You couldn't see him if you wanted to—unless . . .

If you have a Detect Invisibility spell, go to **223**. If you didn't bring a Detect Invisibility spell with you or have no spells left, turn to **196**.

147

You pass through the huge gates and cross a wide, empty courtyard. You can feel a heavy pall of death resting on this place, and you can almost see the ghosts of the past shambling over the ancient stone cobbles. Some seem to stop and watch your passing, nodding their heads knowingly. Do they know who you are and why you are here?

Across the wide courtyard you see the base of the main keep. As you watch, its two doors also swing open, silently beckoning you to enter. With Caramon at your side, you pass through the doors into the black foretower of the inner keep of the Towers of High Sorcery. A long corridor, lit faintly by small glowing globes, leads you to a small, cold chamber. In the center of the chamber sits Par-Salian himself.

He wears the great white robes of his powerful office, which seem to weigh heavily upon him as he sits slightly slumped in his chair. You wonder how old he really is, when the gods will replace him, and what forces the replacement will serve—evil or neutrality or good? He appears to be thinking deeply. Perhaps he might even be asleep.

As you enter the room and approach him, he slowly raises his head and fixes you with an appraising look that stops you in your tracks.

Caramon stops as well and bends to whisper something in your ear. "I thought he was asleep for a second there."

"No," you reply softly. "He's been watching since we entered the forest . . . even sooner, I'll wager."

Your hushed conversation is interrupted by a coughing sound as the ancient mage clears his throat to speak. "Greetings, Raistlin," he begins. His long, gaunt face is strong, framed by thick, surprisingly dark hair streaked with lines of gray. Alert gray eyes look out from deep within his face. From their dark recesses, they glitter as he looks you up and down. "I have been observing you since you entered our valley. You have done well to progress this far."

"Thank you, Great One," you answer in awed tones of respect. "Your messenger was a great help."

"Ah, him!" the mage chuckles. "An old acquaintance of mine. He asked if he could help see you through the barrier. In truth, it was his idea to begin to test you at that point. I trust he wasn't too much of a problem for you?"

"Of course not, Great One," you reply. "His help was most appreciated."

Caramon grunts audibly from behind you, and a knowing smile spreads over Par-Salian's face.

"Well, enough of that. Now that you are here, are you prepared to undergo your Test?" the mage asks softly.

Roll one die and add the result to your presence skill

score. If you saw the face of the spectral minion in the Wayreth Forest, subtract 1 from your die roll. If the total is 7 or more, turn to **26**. If it is 6 or less, turn to **64**.

148

"Well, then," you say. "Let's get on with it, shall we?"

The gang leader begins to circle you warily. You stand and watch for a second or two, then quickly kneel and scoop up a small handful of sand.

"You'll have to do better than that, magician," the bully says. "Do you expect to do us all in with a handful of sand?"

Slowly you rise to your feet, smiling to yourself. Turning around in a complete circle, you carefully pronounce the words of your Sleep spell.

"Ast tasarak simularan krynawi."

In a moment, just as you expected, you hear the sound of heavy snoring and breathing. They have all fallen into a deep sleep.

How convenient! you think. *Asleep so soundly. It would be so easy to simply cut their throats and be rid of them once and for all!*

Slowly you reach for the hilt of your dagger. Suddenly, before your startled eyes, one of the sleeping bullies makes a loud popping sound and disappears in a puff of smoke! Then another and another, until they're all gone!

A short grunt makes you whirl around. The leader is sitting on the ground, looking up at you intently with a scowl on his face. Then he stands and dusts off his pants.

"It wouldn't have been a good idea to try to cut our throats, young mage," he says seriously. "The Shapers of the Test are looking for master mage material, not a murderer. You'd do well to remember that."

128

Quickly you jerk your hand away from the hilt of your knife. Seeing your guilty reaction to his words, he laughs, his face transforming into a broad smile. Turn to **214**.

149

You ponder the great mage's offer for only a moment. You are confident the lending of a small portion of your life is a small price to pay for guaranteed success in the Test and the respect of the world. Your choice is simple.

"Great One," you begin reverently, "you are generous indeed. If I can be of any aid to you, I will most certainly accept your offer."

Besides, you think quickly, *there will come a time when I will turn this trade to my own advantage. Then we shall see what we shall see!*

Fistandantalus chuckles happily. "Excellent!" he says. "I had hoped your natural arrogance would be put aside in the light of reason."

"But when will you call upon me to aid you, Great One?" you ask. "And what about the guarantees you spoke of?"

"Do not concern yourself about when I will call," he replies tightly. "You will know it when I do. As for the aid, I give you two gifts. First," he says with a wave of his hand, "a full complement of spell components. You will find them in your robes. You will be free to use any spell you have at your command during the final phase of the Test. Second, I give you this."

He passes his hand across the front of his body. The air shimmers slightly, then distorts, then finally the distortion solidifies and becomes . . .

"A staff!" you gasp.

"Yes," he says, "the Staff of Magius. I have held it for just such a one as you. Take it, Raistlin. It is yours!"

You gaze in awe at the polished brown wood of the magic staff. One end is covered with metal of some kind. At the other end, you see a claw holding a glass ball.

Anxiously you reach out for the staff. To your surprise, it jumps into your hand! Instantly you know it—what it does, its innate spells, how it can help and protect you.

"Now," says your new mentor, "be off with you. The

fourth phase of the Test awaits you. Remember, together we can conquer anything—even the world of Krynn." He makes an arcane gesture and he is gone. The room slowly fades around you. Turn to **120**.

150

You awaken you know not how much later. The meal you ate put you to sleep faster than you imagined possible. If the food wasn't drugged, then fatigue is a far more powerful narcotic than you ever dreamed.

You blink your eyes as you see something that wasn't there before. Written on the wall opposite you, in large letters, is a message:

If these WORDS you seek to UNDERSTAND,
Their message will lend a PROTECTING hand.

You ponder their meaning for several minutes, but if the message is intended to be a clue, you fail to understand it. Suddenly the message disappears as suddenly as it appeared.

At any rate, it is time now to meditate and memorize the arcane words of the spells in your spellbook. What will be your choices? Will you choose spells that are offensive in nature or will you select defensive spells for the next phase of the Test? Is there some clue in the mysterious message that appeared on the wall? Perhaps a mixture of both would be more appropriate. What spell components have you acquired that can be used for casting those spells? It's hard to tell what the Shapers of the Test have in mind for you and even harder to prepare correctly.

It is time to choose your spells. You may choose only three—two first level spells and one second level spell. Which will they be? You may wish to refer to **10**.

Once you have selected your spells, write their names on the back of your Character Stats Card. You will need to use the components for each spell, if needed, when you cast it.

You may also add 1 point to your hit point total—provided you have lost any—because of the strength you recovered from your rest.

With your spells chosen, it's now time to continue the Test. Once again, you pass through the narrow door and find yourself stepping into the now familiar three-halled corridor. The cleverly hidden secret door disappears into the wall behind you as soon as you close it.

Much to your surprise, however, the short hall leading to the door with the white triangle has disappeared! There remain only two halls and two doors now. *Perhaps someone is trying to make my life a little easier,* you think.

If you decide to try the door with the red triangle, turn to **152**. If you decide to go through the door with the black triangle, turn to **17**.

151

"That sounds all right to me, I guess," your twin grunts, "but you can't seriously ask me to go into that forest, let alone go in yourself, just to take a silly little test. That's foolishness! The place reeks of evil, rotten things! It can't be worth it! I mean, I'm not afraid of anything, but . . . well, curse it all, Raist, we could die in there! I can feel it!"

You stiffen your back ever so slightly at his last thought. *He has hit closer to the mark than I want him to,* you think rapidly. *Curse his fighter's instincts, anyway! I've got to get him off that track, and fast!*

Roll one die and add the result to your presence ability score. If the total is 7 or more, turn to **74**. If it is 6 or less, turn to **191**.

152

You look toward the door with the red triangle on it and recall the words of the poem: *"Blood-red death, ever present, you must fear,"* it said. *This next part of the Test sounds dangerous!*

You approach the door cautiously. Its moldy, wooden slats show many signs of great age. A heavy ring of tarnished metal hangs in the middle of the door. As you lift the ring, it makes a loud screech. It's all you can do to get the door open, and the rusty hinges howl as it swings aside.

On the other side, carved into the mother rock that forms the foundation of the towers, you find a dank stairway leading down into the earth. Two small globes, one on either side of the tunnel, glisten off the walls and stairs of the damp, slimy tunnel. The air smells of death.

That screeching door surely alerted anything that's waiting down there, you think. *So much for the element of surprise.* You start to go down the stairs. Every ten feet or so, another set of globes lights up, providing enough light to see by as you descend.

After about fifty feet, you come to the bottom of the stairs. There is a tunnel leading off to your left and another leading off to your right. On the wall straight across from you hangs a small sign, inscribed with a short verse:

> For those who would rather GIVE than RECEIVE
> Your road lies to the left, I believe.
> But if GIVING is to you a blight,
> Then follow the path that leads to the right.

Giving? Receiving? By the gods, can't these mages ever talk in plain language? I'm tired of riddles.

Roll one die and add the result to your reasoning skill score. If the total is 8 or more, turn to **81**. If it is 7 or less, turn to **101**.

153

The dragonman drops to its hands and feet and begins to charge across the room at you. Before you know what is happening, it is on top of you, and you know you are finished! Turn to **15**.

You decide that your mysterious benefactor wouldn't have left behind a message if it weren't important for you to face the tests in some order. It seems, then, that you must somehow try to connect the red, white, and black doors with the past, present, and future. But which color represents which time period?

Roll one die and add the result to your reasoning skill score. If the total sum is less than 7, turn to **192**. If it is 7 or more, turn to **208**.

155

As the leader's right-hand man starts to hurl the club, you whisper tersely to the leader standing before you. "Stop him!"

The leader spins about just as the club flies at you. Deftly, he reaches out and catches it in one hand. Brandishing the club threateningly, he advances toward his comrade.

"I'll give you all fair warning," he shouts, turning to address them all. "If any of you harm so much as a hair on this man's head, I'll split your own head with this club! Now, be off with you! My friend and I have something to discuss, and we don't want any undesirables about while we're talking. Scram!"

Startled by his sudden change, his followers turn and disappear into the woods.

Suddenly you hear loud laughter. For a moment, you think you may have misjudged your opponent and he is about to betray you. Instead you see the young man standing before you, the smile on his face even wider now. But you can tell that he has recovered from the effect of your spell. Turn to **214**.

156

Another wave of boundless terror sweeps over you as the shrouded figure approaches. Fear tears at your mind, making it almost impossible even to think.

Test your reasoning by rolling one die and adding the result to your reasoning skill score. If the total is 9 or more, turn to **106**. If it is 8 or less, turn to **22**.

157

A cruel chuckle echoes across the cavern. Already the drow has begun to cast another spell, but you hardly hear the words it utters. You know you are beaten.

The acknowledgement of defeat has left you numb, and with that acknowledgement comes a terrible realization, an idea so shocking you are shaken beyond any pain.

You somehow know that you were not meant to win! This has all been a cruel joke! The Shapers of the Test have let you get this far, only to jerk victory from your grasp.

You barely see the finger of flame stream from the drow's hand. You don't even feel it touch your chest and explode into a ball of fire. Turn to **25**.

158

This is the opening that Caramon has been waiting for! Without hesitation, he leaps at the monster. He lands squarely on the beast's shoulders and locks his powerful legs around its neck. Before the creature knows what is happening, Caramon slams his sword point down into its brain.

Once more Caramon howls his war cry. With animal ferocity, he shoves on the blade with all his weight until the blade, with the beast's skewered head, is buried deep in the ground.

You move to your twin brother's side, and the two of you exchange knowing glances. Once again you have triumphed as a team.

But as you stand over the monster's inert body, a cold, icy voice enters your thoughts. It seems to originate from the forest.

"Well done, my fine young men!" the voice begins. "We hope you will forgive the inconvenience, but on occasion one of our watchers becomes overzealous in the pursuit of its duty. You have seen the result. The outcome is not always so favorable for travelers such as yourselves."

The speaker pauses momentarily. A soft, icy chuckle sends shivers up and down your spine. Then the voice continues.

"But now, seeker of the Test, we invite you to enter our humble abode. We await within the forest . . . to flail the meat from your miserable bones and pluck your eyes from their sockets. We long to taste your blood as we have tasted that of so many others. Come! Come!"

The voice fills your mind with cold dread. Never have you heard a sound so full of sinister foreboding. Yet a path through the forest has been opened for you. Is it nothing more than a trap set to destroy you?

Caramon glances at you nervously and awaits your decision. He has said that he will go with you, but it is clear that he wants to go home.

If you decide to brave the forest path, turn to **188**. If, however, you feel certain that the path is a trap and want to seek a way around the forest, turn to **14**.

159

"I have chosen my spells, Master Par-Salian, and my spellbook will be with me should I require any others."

"Excellent," the master mage replies, more to the air than to you. "I hope they'll cover the situations you'll meet." He is not smiling now. Instead, the atmosphere in the room has become very tense.

"You realize, of course, that your brother cannot stay with you," Par-Salian reminds you. "He will be well cared for in your absence, and he will also be allowed to carry home your valuables in the event the test proves to be beyond your skills."

"Carry home valuables?" Caramon asks, bewildered. "You mean—?"

"Yes, dear brother," you cut in sharply. "Par-Salian means that you will be allowed to take home my belongings should I meet my death during the Test." *A great likelihood,* you think. "That should be fairly easy for even you to understand."

"You must understand that failure invariably proves fatal," interjects Par-Salian.

"Look, Raist," says Caramon, his voice trembling, "perhaps you should forget about him. Why don't we just go home?" Placing his hand on your shoulder, Caramon continues. "Please, Raist. I'm supposed to take care of you."

"No!" you thunder at him, wrenching away from his touch. "This is my battle, and I will fight it! Be gone, and leave me to fight my own battles!" Your tone leaves no room for argument.

"All right, Raist, all right," he mumbles. "I'll meet you outside . . . later." He shoots a threatening glance at the mage and departs.

After Caramon has departed, you turn to Par-Salian. "I apologize for my brother's conduct, Great One," you mutter.

"Why should you apologize?" the mage asks.

"Well, he lacks a certain degree of—of understanding. Now, can't we just get on with this?"

"Of course," Par-Salian says, leaning back in his high-backed chair. "But remember this, young man. Your test has been designed to gauge not only your magical prowess but your grasp of certain valuable lessons of life. The Shapers of the Test hope that you may learn something from it. But be warned that your ultimate success will depend to a great degree on how wisely you use your experience to see you through your trials, and on how well you face up to them. Cowardice could be disastrous! Failure to face up to any part of the Test will almost certainly mean death! Never forget that!

"I must also warn you that there is a presence, a certain being, not of this plane or time, who is very concerned about you and your chances of success. He may well try to influence some of your decisions during the Test. You would do well to consider carefully whatever words of counsel or advice he may offer you. Following his advice may not always reward you with what you seek. Now, be gone!"

You look at the master mage one last time, and he casually gestures behind you. The air around you suddenly thickens and seems to freeze. You have just enough time to suck in a quick breath before a rush of cold envelops you and chills you to your very bones. Then a crack of thunder reverberates through the room, and the chamber evaporates into darkness . . . for a while.

Turn to **85**.

160

Your mind and body respond like lightning. Summoning the magical forces of the towers, you face the monster roaring defiantly before you. As the power surges through you, you begin to utter the words of the first spell you are going to cast.

Turn to **10**. Cross-index the line containing the spell you wish to cast with the column corresponding to this section number. The number at the junction of these two columns is the number of the section you must turn to to see how your spell works.

161

Inky blackness begins to surround you. You know this drow, with its infravision, is sure to defeat you in the darkness. If you don't do something in the next few seconds, you are doomed! Your skills and experience now face their ultimate test!

Roll one die and add the result to your agility skill score. If you can get a total of 9, including any experience points you may choose to spend, turn to **57**. If the total is less than 9, turn to **89**.

162

You simply can't think clearly! In desperation, you pull your hidden dagger from your robes. *This will put an end to this spectre's mockery!* you think. Taking deadly aim, you fling the blade through the air at your foe's chest.

The fog around you explodes in laughter. You look at your opponent. The blade has passed harmlessly straight through him! He, too, is shaking with uncontrolled laughter! That laughter, a weird, shrill, mocking sound, pierces

you to the core. It testifies of your failure. There is no hope. Your strength is spent.

You have lost.

As this realization sinks into your heart, your enemy suddenly thrusts his right hand toward you and clenches his fist. The laughter increases to a screaming crescendo, smothering you in derision.

As the spectre draws his hand toward his face, you are pulled irresistibly toward him. Across the clearing he pulls you, until you stand only a few feet in front of him. He holds you in his thrall, letting the laughter wash over you with full effect.

Suddenly he drives his fist down toward the ground. Your knees buckle and snap loudly as you are forced to kneel before him. The pain in your legs and your humiliation are overwhelming, and the thunderous laughter from the mists shatters your hearing, burying you under its sound as it reverberates inside your head. Turn to **97**.

163

You are stunned! Fistandantalus himself! The greatest, most powerful mage in the history of Krynn! A mage so adept that he was able to transcend the known bounds of magic and call up powers and forces unknown to any other. How else could he have leveled the Dwarfgate Plain and destroyed both the contending armies, not to mention— *himself!* You realize with a start that this man is supposed to be dead!

"Yes, I'm supposed to be dead," chuckles Fistandantalus, reading the shocked look on your face just as clearly as if he'd read your mind. "That is why we are here, on another plane. That is also why you are here. I have a proposition to offer you regarding the life and death of both of us. But first, come close and you and I will review what you have done."

You draw close to the legendary mage. When you are within his reach, he leans forward and extends his hand. His fingers touch your forehead and temples gently, and as they do, an amazing thing happens. You find yourself reliving the Test in every detail! The forest, the bullies in Solace, the cleric Verminaard, the dragonmen—everything you experienced passes through your mind.

Fistandantalus's soft voice brings you back to the present. "Now, young mage," he whispers, "let us see if you have used your experience wisely and gained anything from the Test so far."

The weight of Fistandantalus's judgment is based on the number of experience points you have remaining at this point in the Test. If you have 5 or more experience points left, turn to **62**. If you have 3 or 4 experience points remaining, go to **29**. If you have less than 3 experience points left, turn to **203**.

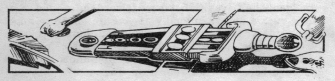

164

It seems to you that the only way to get Caramon to cooperate is to keep him from guessing the truth. *If he ever found out what awaits me in there,* you think, *he'd never allow me to enter. All would be lost. I will have to feign ignorance.*

"Brother, I am at a loss to explain why this forest is here. I am as befuddled by its appearance as you are. But it is here, and I'm sure that the Test I seek lies somewhere beyond it, perhaps even inside the forest itself."

You pause shortly as you consider appealing to his adventurous warrior nature. "It certainly represents a challenge, don't you think? I'm sure that once we find a way in, we'll not only discover some clue to further my quest, but we'll also have ourselves a rousing good adventure as well. Shall we get on with it?"

Roll one die and add the result to your presence skill score. If the total is 8 or more, turn to **182**. If it is 7 or less, turn to **191**. Remember, if you think it's important enough, you can add experience points to any die roll. If you decide to use any experience points, be sure to decide how many points you wish to spend and subtract them from your total experience points, whether your die roll is successful or not.

165

The voice chuckles softly. "Young mage, you are in no position to demand anything of me . . . at present. But believe me, should you pass this Test, you may well be able to ask of me anything your heart could desire. As for seeing me, that will come in good time. Do not fret for now. Be warned, though, that the circumstances of my appearance will not be the most pleasant. But now your attention is required in a far more weighty matter—your own survival. Behold!"

Turn to **215**.

166

The raging explosion of flame swirls around you. The heat whips your robes and hair about your face as though you were standing in a hurricane. All around you, the darkness fades. The walls are scorched by the heat.

But, miraculously, you remain unscathed! You stand in the midst of the terrifying conflagration—and it doesn't do a thing to you!

Suddenly everything stops. Movement simply freezes in place and time. You dimly see the drow across the cavern, its mouth agape in amazement. The flames cease to rage about you.

Then a voice pierces your mind. "Now, Raistlin," it whispers, "now is our bargain to be completed I have saved you from certain death. That you can plainly see."

A shining silvery panel materializes before you. Your eyes widen in amazement as you gasp at the visage in the mirror.

Your skin, once tanned and normal, is now a gleaming, metallic golden color. Your hair is bleached white!

"No, you will never look the same," husks the voice of Fistandantalus. "But those were the steps necessary to preserve your life. However, you've more to worry about than your appearance. Look to your enemy. The drow is only momentarily held. You must deal with it before it can free itself. Then we will conclude our agreement!"

If you have the staff, turn to **194**. If you have the scroll, go to **67**.

167

The two smaller dragonmen drop to a crouching position and begin to flap their wings as they run on all fours, almost flying in your direction! Before you can begin to utter the words of a spell, they are swarming all over you.

A claw whips out and knocks your hands to one side. Another lashes out and smashes your head against the wall. In a daze, you feel a toothy snout close over your throat and squeeze slowly. You struggle to free yourself, reaching in vain for your concealed dagger, but thick, scaly arms bind your arms to your body. Soon the air in your lungs is gone, and your mind goes blank.

Turn to **15**.

168

These low-lifes! you think with a sneer. *How dare they think they can stand up to me? I'll show them a thing or two,* you vow.

Knowing bullies to be the cowards they are, you decide you have two choices of action.

If you decide to try to scare them into submission with a bluff, turn to **87**. If you prefer not to waste any more time on these bullies and choose to defend yourself with a spell, turn to **197**.

Dimly, through the lifting fog, you begin to see the outline of a huge structure, reaching into the air from the ground like a huge taloned claw. As the mists clear, your heart pounds within your chest. You have arrived at your destination—the Towers of High Sorcery, walled and shimmering with magic, loom before you!

Immense black walls seem to grow right out of the ground in front of you. Huge runic symbols are carved deep into the walls, adding powerful magic spells to the formidable strength of the stone itself. Nothing known to the world of Krynn could ever penetrate them, you think—nothing, that is, short of another Cataclysm.

The very nature of this fabled place makes your skin creep. The towers, the Test, and your growing fears all make you begin to doubt your confidence.

Make a presence check here. Roll one die and add the result to your presence skill score. If you saw the face of the spectral minion while you were in the Wayreth Forest, subtract 1 from your die roll. If your total is 6 or more, turn to **147**. If it is less, turn to **70**.

Fistandantalus has offered you guaranteed success in return for a portion of your life-force. You think about his offer carefully. It's tempting indeed.

But something about the offer and the mage bothers you. Perhaps it's his attitude, perhaps his clandestine manipulation of your Test. Maybe it's his unspoken belief that you can't succeed on your own.

That last one rankles you! You've gotten this far with precious little help from him; you can complete the Test without him as well!

"Great One," you begin, "I appreciate your concern for my well-being, but I find your offer unacceptable. Better I trust in Gilean and my own resources than outside aid! Besides, I need all my life-force to stay alive."

Fistandantalus straightens slowly in his throne and gazes at you for long seconds. You wonder momentarily if you should retract your bold statement, but before you can speak again, he stands abruptly.

"Even I had not thought you could be so arrogant!" he hisses vehemently. "Go then, and face the end alone. I will even give you a full complement of spell components. You will find them in your robe. You will be free to use any spell at your command. Let us see how you, your gods, and your vaunted 'resources' stand up in the face of death!"

With a flick of his hand, he disappears and the room fades around you. Turn to **120**.

171

You realize fully the danger of what you plan to do. This spell will bring you within striking range of the beast. But your brother is in extreme danger, and you must concentrate fully on the spell you are about to cast.

Thumbs together, you advance toward the ogredog, whose attention is focused on Caramon. Your brother continues to hold its attention, but you know he can't keep it up much longer. The ogredog tenses its body for an attack.
Just a few more inches . . . now!

Arcane words flow from your lips. Magic forces course through your body, causing tongues of fire to leap from your outstretched fingers, bathing the hindquarters of the beast in flames. With a yelp of pain and a howl of rage, the giant monster whirls around. One massive paw lashes out toward you and sends you sprawling. Slowly grinding its jaws, the ogredog begins advancing toward you. Subtract 2 hit points from your total and turn to **158**.

172

"*. . . kalith karan, tobanis kar!*"

The final words of your Magic Missile spell pass your lips, and two glittering darts of white light form at your fingertips. Concentrating intensely, you send them streaking across the room, one for each dragonman who stands over

144

the little dwarf.

With a burst of light, they hit exactly on target. The impact is strong enough to break their necks, and they crumple to the ground, dead.

There is a loud cheer from the gully dwarves. The lead dragonman is momentarily stunned, but it recovers quickly. Leaving the dwarves to swarm out of the pot and escape through the tunnels, it grabs for its belt. Looking directly at the tunnel you are standing in, it pulls a small object from a pouch at its belt. Mumbling a few words to itself, it steps over to the hole and disappears from sight.

Roll one die and add the result to your reasoning skill score. If the total is 8 or more, turn to **146**. If it's less than 8, turn to **37**.

173

"Very well, then," rasps the voice, "I will tell you some little about myself. It cannot be much, however. There are many years and much distance between us, and it is very difficult for me to communicate with you on your plane. I must be brief.

"Your success will have far-reaching consequences," the voice continues, "perhaps even on the very future of life on Krynn. There is much more at stake here than you can possibly imagine. You should also know that I have a vested interest in your success."

"But who are you, and what do you want of me?" you repeat in a whisper.

"My name is unimportant—for now. As for what I want of you, that is easily explained. I need your power to aid me in a very important task. In return, I can insure that you pass the Test. You see, I know what is in store for you, and you can believe me when I say you will be lucky to survive. But survive you must! I will see to that!"

"But what if I don't need or want your help? And do Par-Salian or the Shapers of the Test know of your interference?" you ask. "This hardly seems proper."

"What do you know of 'proper'?" the voice hisses. "And do not be too sure of your abilities. It would be foolhardy indeed to refuse help that could mean the difference between life and death. Besides, I myself am one of the Shapers of your Test. As I said, I have a personal interest in your success. Look for my aid in time of great need, though I will arrive when I deem it necessary. But enough of this. There are more important matters at hand—namely your survival. Behold!"

Turn to **215**.

174

Strands of thick webbing grow from the ceiling and floor to entrap your enemy. The drow soon finds itself standing in a forest of spiderweb!

The evil creature just stands and laughs. Then, as easily as waving a hand, it spreads its arms and brushes your webs aside.

A sinking feeling spreads through you. There's nothing you can do to this creature. It's magic-resistant! Turn to **157**.

175

Your brother's painful defeat at the hands of the spectral minion leaves you stunned, even though you suspected what would happen. Now all you can do is stand there, fearful that the minion may choose next to demonstrate his power to you. Even the sight of Caramon writhing in pain isn't enough to get you to move.

The spectre looks toward you once more. Shaking his head slowly, he crosses the clearing to stand in front of you.

You lower your eyes. By some sixth sense, you know what is coming. You are ashamed and afraid.

When the spectre finally speaks, his voice is thick with reproach. "And you pretend to be ready to take the Test!" he scoffs. "You who cannot even conquer your fear enough to go to the aid of your brother. I warn you now, Raistlin, that such fear will be the death of you during the Test. Luckily for you, it is not my mission to destroy you. I was sent to test you and, if necessary, to teach you a lesson. That I will now do. Look at me, Raistlin, and see what the future holds for you!" Turn to **145**.

176

A fan-shaped spray of flames shoots from your outstretched hands, searing your opponent's face.

He screams horribly as the fire burns into his eyes, and he falls to the ground, howling in pain and beating at his flaming clothes and hair.

Unfortunately, the rest of the plan doesn't work as you thought it would. You barely have time to see a flicker of movement before a club catches you square in the ribs, cracking one of them with a loud snap. Another club catches you soundly behind the ear. As you collapse to the ground, more blows from fists and feet hammer you into unconsciousness.

Subtract 3 points from your hit point total and turn to **219**.

177

"OOF!"

The words of your spell still incomplete, two hundred and fifty pounds of flying warrior slam into your side and knock you to the ground. As you try to recover your breath, Caramon plants himself squarely on top of your chest, one hand clamped over your mouth and his knees pinning your arms to the ground. He has an enraged look in his eyes as he glares down at you, but when he speaks, his voice is heavy with hurt.

"A spell!" he exclaims. "You tried to use a spell—on me! Have you forgotten who has fought at your side for all these months? Well, let me tell you something, *little* brother. I haven't spent all this time looking out for you just to have you march merrily into the jaws of death. We're heading for home right now, and that's final!"

With a strength made even greater by anger and hurt, he springs to his feet and tosses you effortlessly over his shoulder.

"Caramon, you oaf!" you shout, enraged. "Put me down—*now! I must* go to the towers. Don't you understand? If you don't let me go through with the Test, my whole life will have been wasted. Now I command you—*put me down!*"

Your brother pauses briefly and his muscles seem to relax. He seems to be pondering your words. You start to squirm out of his grasp. Turn to **30**.

178

I'd better not to leave anything to chance, you think. *I'll check the table as well. There may be something there I can use.*

You move over to the table and look over its contents. A small, sooty burner sits in one corner of the table. Resting on top of the burner is a flint and some string. Hanging on a nail at the edge of the table by the burner is a small pail of coal. Fastened to the other corner of the table stands a miniature grinding wheel. Its mechanism appears to be a bit rusty, but it still seems to work. Next to the wheel you see a crystalline jar containing rods of amber, glass, bronze, steel, and some other substances you don't recognize.

A clay vase of red roses and white daisies occupies the middle of the table. You also find a few pieces of parchment beneath a jar of copper pieces. Looking beneath the table, you notice nothing but a small drum and a few spiders and spiderwebs.

It's a good thing no one has cleaned up, you think. There are still plenty of things I can make use of here.

Choosing from the items mentioned above and referring to **10** if you wish, write down the rest of the components you wish to bring along with you on the back of your Character Stats Card. Remember, you are limited to four components in all, so make sure you can make use of what you take.

Now, having chosen your spell components, you settle down to the sumptuous meal left for you by the Ki-rin. It's more than enough to fill, and you soon drift off to sleep. Turn to **150**.

179

You stand over the inert body of the drow. Almost beyond belief, it is finally dead and you have won!

The magnitude of it suddenly overwhelms you. No matter that you were saved from disaster by the greatest mage the world of Krynn has ever known. You have won! You are still alive! And the respect of the world is yours—as well as this incredible staff!

Your spirit soars like a great bird free upon the winds. No words can tell of your elation and joy. You can barely contain it yourself, almost passing out in ecstasy at the thrill.

But even as you reach the peak of elation, you are struck down. Like a thunderbolt from heaven, a force hits you! It grabs at you, passes around you, tears at you.

As the force passes, you feel something inside you being torn away. Some part of what must be your soul is wrenched violently from your being. So painful is the parting that you scream in agony and fall to your knees. A wracking cough convulses our trembling body, and blood spatters the floor as you cough again. You feel as though your insides have been ripped to shreds.

From the air around you, thunder crashes. "Our bargain is complete!" booms a voice.

You fall to your face on the floor beneath the weight of that vaguely familiar voice. In a moment, you realize that it belongs to Fistandantalus! But now it sounds different. It's full of strength and life—*your* life! Turn to **226**.

Below the great arch that supports the doors leading into the towers stands the hooded figure you encountered at the edge of the Wayreth Forest. The spectral minion stands with his arms folded across his chest, but as you approach, he raises one hand.

The horses nearly bolt once more, but having felt his icy presence once, they are somewhat easier to control.

The spectre's hollow voice echoes across the space between you, seeming to almost freeze the surrounding air.

"Who dares approach the Towers of High Sorcery? State your business. If it be of note to those within, you may live and pass inside. If not, prepare to meet your death here and now!"

Roll one die and add the result to your presence skill score. Remember, if you saw the face of the spectral minion in the forest, you must subtract 1 from your die roll. If the total is 5 or more, go to **11**. If it is less than 5, turn to **104**.

181

Enraged, the ogre mage roars in anger. He punches the crystalline door with his clenched fist. The door is thrown open against you. You are slammed breathless to one side. As you struggle for air, he reaches through the portal. A huge meaty claw grabs you by the robes and drags you into the chamber. You strive frantically to escape, but he has too

sure a hold on you. Clasping you in both claws, he raises you slowly up to his mouth. You struggle uselessly in his powerful grip. You flail at his claws, trying to deny that your chance to become a great mage is going to end at the bottom of this creature's stomach. The beast's foul, putrid breath washes over you.

The scream that tears from your throat is lost in his hungry, black maw.

Go to **18**.

182

"All right, Raist," Caramon says slowly. "You will prevail in this matter. If you say you have to go in there, we'll go in, even though I don't like it. I guess someone's got to be there to pull your bacon out of the fire if you get in trouble." He laughs at his joke, and then turns back to prepare your horses.

You answer very softly, keeping a tight rein on your feelings. "Thank you, Caramon. I'm always glad to have your aid."

But deep inside, your thoughts roil in anger. *Pull my bacon out of the fire, indeed! I can stand on my own, dear brother, and this Test will prove it, once and for all! And even if the Test should lay claim to my life, there would be nothing you could do to save me.*

Caramon returns with your horse, interrupting your thoughts. "Let's get going, Raist. The sooner we get this over with, the better."

As you mount your horse, you glance at your warrior brother again. You realize suddenly that, despite your resentment, you care for him a great deal.

Then you slowly turn back toward the Wayreth Forest. *Death may await me in there,* you think. *Perhaps death awaits both of us. Do I want to be responsible for Caramon's death as well as my own?* Incredibly, now that you are free to enter the wood, you aren't sure that it's the best course of action.

Roll one die and add the result to your presence ability score. If the total is 5 or more, turn to **36**. If it is 4 or less, go to **14**.

183

Murmuring softly, you chant your Darkness spell over the tiny lump of coal you hold in your hand. You watch in satisfaction as a deep, inky black mist slowly begins to fill the room.

The gathering blackness has a dramatic, and puzzling, effect on the dragonmen. They immediately begin to look about wildly, as though expecting to hear or see something. The one with the whip drops it to the ground and begins to shake visibly. Its companion falls to the ground and starts to slaver and convulse in fear. The leader drops its mace, falls to its knees, and throws its claws in front of its face. You hear it shriek something in a strange hissing language before darkness surrounds it.

Puzzled by the bizarre reactions of the dragonmen, you can only guess that powerful magic has somehow augmented your spell.

As the darkness in the room becomes complete, the light from the sconces is quenched. You can see nothing, but you hear strange hissing screams from the three creatures. They rise to a crescendo, then suddenly recede. Finally the room is silent.

In a few short minutes, the darkness begins to dissipate. As it leaves, all you see is the little body of the gully dwarf lying on the floor. The rest of the room is completely empty. The pot is gone, the dragonmen vanished.

Suddenly you feel very strange. You look up to see the walls of the chamber beginning to shimmer with a strange, iridescent light, as if some powerful magic is at work! Turn to **123**.

It can't hit me if it can't tell where I am! you think rapidly.

Swiftly you murmur your Mirror Image spell. In seconds, there are four of you! You and your images advance toward the drow to get in range for your next spell.

But the drow is muttering the words of its own spell. Before you can react with a counterspell, three Magic Missiles shoot from its fingers. Two of them pass into two of your images, and they vanish. The third hits you in the chest!

Many times you have used a Magic Missile spell on others, but you've never felt its sting yourself—until now! Even as the pain lances along your nerves, three more magic missiles slide off your opponent's fingertips. Two slam into the last of your images, which pops from sight, but the last missile hits you.

The pain is excruciating. Your vision clouds as pain fills your eyes with a red haze. Turn to **157**.

Your desire to face the Test and claim its rewards far outweighs any fears you have of this place. To try to take your mind off these nagging doubts, you think of the history of Krynn and its wizards. You realize that Caramon knows virtually nothing about the towers.

"Let me tell you something about the Towers of High Sorcery, Caramon," you begin. "The walls you see are some one hundred feet thick at their base, gradually narrowing to thirty at the top—completely impenetrable. It is said that they are built right into the bedrock. And do you see those strange inscriptions carved into the walls? Those are powerful, age-old wards created by the Ancients themselves to give supernatural strength to the stone."

"But why would they need supernatural strength?" asks your brother. "Who would ever want to attack a place like this?"

"At one time, the people of Krynn rose up in revolt against the mages and began to attack them and their sanctuaries," you explain. "At that time, most such magical strongholds were destroyed. This is the only one of its kind that remains. It is the last abode of the great mages of Krynn. It was built to stand for countless ages and withstand anything."

Caramon stares in wide-eyed amazement at the imposing structure. Finally he mumbles, "Why does it shimmer so?"

"That is magic, Caramon. In all of Krynn, you will never stand in a place where the magical forces of this plane are more concentrated. They all center here. Some even say that certain of the other planes of existence touch here as well."

As the last wisps of mist evaporate from around the towers, you find yourselves nearing the main gate. Your attention is fixed on the huge oaken doors with their rune-inscribed steel bindings.

A familiar chill passes over you as the great doors swing silently outward, opening mystically to greet you. Turn to **180**.

186

The past be hanged! you think angrily. Your sense of justice will not be turned aside. You *must* make these people aware of the danger they are in.

"Are you so blind that you can't see the danger you are in?" you shout above the crowd. "This man would have you cast aside your long-standing beliefs in favor of gods that have proved nothing to you. He tells you that the new gods will require much of you. He will have you satisfying those gods by human sacrifice before you know it, perhaps even before this day is over. Yet he says nothing of what they will give you in return! In short, he's a fraud and a fake and will lead you all to ruin!"

You pause to seek a reaction to your words, but you are answered by nothing but stunned silence. Turn to **23**.

187

You manage to finish the words of your spell before the ogre can react. But to your dismay, your spell fizzles out as it hits the door. It has absolutely no effect inside the chamber, where the ogre now stands roaring in anger! You realize this was definitely the wrong spell to try to use, now of all times. Turn to **181**.

188

"We will enter!" you shout toward the forest.

"Are you crazy?" Caramon snaps. "We're dead men if we go in there!"

"Take heart, brother. Did you not see how the forest opened for me? They are clearing a path to ease our journey. It would be in poor taste to refuse their generous offer. Have no fear, Caramon. I will be at your side. Trust me!"

Turning, you address the fog-enshrouded voice. "It is indeed most gracious of you to provide us a way to enter this fearsome wood. We extend our humblest thanks."

The voice breaks into a soft, hissing chuckle as you urge your mount forward toward the path.

Caramon holds back for a moment. "Blast you anyway, Raistlin!" he cries. "You never did show any good sense . . . or caution!" He prods his horse viciously to catch up with you, and the fog swirls to envelop you both as you enter the enchanted wood. Turn to **66**.

189

You rise to your feet before Fistandantalus. He looks at you intently for a while.

"You have done well," he says at last, "given what you had at your disposal. You have proven yourself to be an accomplished and worthy mage. So impressed am I, in fact, that I am going to give you a gift that I had earlier withheld. You have certainly earned it!" He passes his hand across his body in the air. The air shimmers, then seems to congeal, then solidifies into a staff. You stand spellbound.

"It is the Staff of Magius," says Fistandantalus, "a powerful weapon in the hands of a worthy bearer. You will be that bearer. Take it. It is yours!"

You reach out for the staff in awe. To your amazement, it leaps into your hand. As you grab it, an amazing transformation occurs. In an instant, you know this magic item—what it does, what spells it possesses, how it will serve and protect you.

"Let it be a reminder of the bond between us," says the great mage. "Now go and look upon your vanquished foe. Enjoy the fruits of victory. Then we will seal our pact." Turn to **179**.

190

As the ogre mage steps forward to push open the door, four exact images of you appear, side by side. The huge monster steps back, unsure which of you is the right one. Then it shouts the same unintelligible phrase once more.

Since the ogre isn't coming after you at the moment, you have time to cast another spell by turning to **10**. However, if you have used all three of your spells and still don't understand what the ogre mage is trying to tell you, turn to **181**.

Caramon looks at the forest and then at you. Then, slowly and very deliberately, he walks over to where you stand and looks you squarely in the eye.

"Raistlin," he says, "I'm your brother. I've lived with you for a long time. I know just by the sound of your voice that you're hiding something from me. Now I think you'd better tell me what's going on here, or I may have to take matters into my own hands."

His tone leaves no room for misunderstanding. You are certain you know what he means by "taking matters into his own hands." But you must enter that forest!

"Caramon," you say, keeping your voice low and deadly serious, "there are some things that are better left unknown. This is one of them. Be that as it may, I am going into that forest, with or without you!"

You turn sharply and head for your horse. Too stunned to respond immediately, Caramon just stands there. As you reach your horse, you hear him speak, his voice tight with anger.

"*Little* brother," he says huskily, "you are not going anywhere where you might get killed, and most especially not into that forest!" You spin about to see him heading toward you.

Roll one die and add your agility skill score to the result. If the total is 6 or more, turn to **52**. If it is 5 or less, go to **198**.

192

You decide that it makes little or no difference which of the doors you begin with. Nothing in the message seems to indicate what any of the symbols mean. They probably don't have any bearing on the Test at all. With that thought, you begin to move toward one of the doors.

If you choose to enter the door with the white triangle, turn to **99**. If you choose the door with the black triangle, go to **80**. If you elect to go through the door with the red triangle, turn to **204**.

193

In the world of magic, many things can be forgiven. Brashness and forgetfulness are two of these. They can be overcome with age and wisdom and experience.

But one thing that cannot be forgiven is incompetence. Trying to cast a spell without the correct spell component—which you just tried to do—is considered gross incompetence. Gross incompetence usually results in the death of the magic-user!

If you are facing the ogre now, turn to **181**. If you are facing the dragonmen, go to **167**.

194

As Fistandantalus's voice fades, time begins to flow once again. Protected as you now are from the swirling flame of the drow's fireball, the fire passes around you harmlessly. As it does, your plan of attack crystallizes in your brain. The command word for the Continual Light spell in the Staff of Magius leaps into your mind.

"*Shirak!*" you shout.

The ball at the end of your staff erupts in an explosion of light, bathing the cavern in midday brightness.

The drow is virtually crippled by the brilliant light. It screeches in agony and staggers backward, clawing at its eyes as though they were burning within their sockets.

Next you cast your Magic Missile spell. The gleaming white darts streak across the room. With a vengeance, they hit the drow's head and throat and slam it against the wall.

Before the reeling drow can begin to recover from that attack, you send sticky strands of web from the wall and floor to enwrap him. Your Web spell soon has the drow helplessly bound to the wall, unable to move.

You walk across the chamber slowly. The drow glares at you through squinting eyes as it struggles to get to its feet. All it can do is spit contemptuously at you.

That is the drow's last act. In a sweeping arc, your staff crashes through its skull and into its brain. The drow slumps lifelessly against its web coffin.

Turn to **179**.

195

Test your reasoning skill at this point. Roll one die and add the result to your reasoning skill score. If the total is 9 or more, go to **76**. If it is less than 9, turn to **162**.

196

As you try frantically to decide what to do about the invisible dragonman, you catch a faint flicker of movement off to your left. Suddenly, behind you, the lead dragonman reappears! You get one look into its glittering, beady eyes before its heavy steel mace smacks the side of your head with a loud crack and everything goes black. Subtract 6 points from your hit point total and turn to **15**.

197

You count eight of these bullies surrounding you in a circle about twenty feet across.

You glance about and assess the situation quickly. *If I'm going to use a spell,* you think rapidly, *it will have to be one*

*that will get them all at once. Otherwise the rest will be on
me and make short work of me.*

Turn to **136**.

198

"Hold on there, brother," you say soothingly. "I can see
that you won't be satisfied with anything less than the
truth. Well, you deserve that much. I'll have to be a little
more . . . uh, specific in my explanation."

Caramon stops in his tracks. "That's more like it," he
says. "It's about time you saw to reason."

You see him relax a little and fold his arms across his
chest, waiting for you to continue. You move a few more
feet away from him in order to give yourself room and time
to cast your most persuasive spell—Charm Person. *I'm
sorry to have to do this, Caramon,* you think, *but it's the
only way I can be sure that you will cooperate with me. Perhaps it will be better this way. . . .*

"Now listen very carefully, Caramon," you say aloud. "I
am going to tell you just what will happen and how you will
help me." Under your breath, you begin to chant the words
of the spell: *"Tan-tago Mushalah, tan-tago . . ."*

Turn to **177**.

199

The cavern you see before you is about fifty feet across
and roughly circular, almost like an arena. Torches at
either end cast a dim light across the cavern. The roof,

if there is one, is lost in shadow somewhere above you. You have the distinct feeling that someone might be looking at you.

Your senses gather all this information in a fleeting second's time. That's all you have—before your eyes suddenly lock on your opponent.

Your heart sinks as you realize it's a drow—one of the dark elves from legend. You stare at it incredulously. You know of these creatures and how powerful they are from your studies. You also realize what Fistandantalus meant when he said this trial would be very difficult.

You have no time for further contemplation, however, for at almost the same instant you see it, it turns and sees you. It smiles broadly, its teeth shining in its dark face, and faces you full on. Its dark skin glistens in the torchlight, and sweat drips from its light hair and runs down its temples. Its armor gleams dull black in the dim light. A sword and small crossbow hang at its belt.

Immediately it pulls out bat fur and coal from its tunic. It's already halfway through its spell before you even real-

ize what is happening!

Roll one die and add the result to your presence skill score. Remember to subtract 1 from your die roll if you saw the face of the spectral minion, Fistandantalus, in the Wayreth Forest. If the total is 6 or more and you also have the Staff of Magius, turn to **19**. If you get 6 or more and have the scroll, turn to **102**. If the total is 6 or more but you have neither the staff nor the scroll, turn to **161**. If your total is less than 6, no matter what you may have, go to **89**.

200

You seem to be drifting aimlessly in darkness. After some time—does time pass for the dead?—you hear a sound. At first it sounds like a soft chuckle, or perhaps the wind blowing over the sand. Presently it grows more distinct, and you realize that the dust-filled voice has returned.

"Well, well," it begins. "What do you think of death, Raistlin? Not a very pleasant experience, eh?"

"No . . ." you mutter thickly. Then, as the haze in your mind begins to clear somewhat, you say agitatedly, "What is the meaning of this? Why are you playing games with me? Is this all part of my Test, or merely some fickleness on your part?"

"Know, young mage," whispers the dusty voice harshly, "that no 'fickleness' is intended. Since so much depends on you and the outcome of this Test, we are in deadly earnest. I arranged this little demonstration to show you the fruits of failure. Use this experience as a lesson of the nature of your trials. Be they illusory or real, they can kill. I also wanted to see if you could—and would—listen when aid was offered to you. You will be amazed at the power that will be available to you in the very near future if you will just reach out for it!"

The voice chuckles again. "Do not worry for your life. now. You are injured, but not dead. Now, once more, I ask you to listen. I want you to fill your mind with the sensation of lying in a warm stone corridor. Concentrate on that corridor and soon you will be there. Then we will proceed anew."

The voice fades from your hearing. You know now that it

has spoken the truth, and you know that somehow you will have enough strength to continue. You press your eyelids closed and try to concentrate on the security of a warm stone corridor, as the voice suggested.

Subtract 4 points from your hit point total and turn to **141**.

201

The leader of the gang of ruffians returns your stare evenly. With a wicked glint in his eye, he spits out his answer to your warning.

"I don't believe a word of it, charlatan. You weren't that good then and I'm not afraid of you now. Besides, your arm is shaking. Scared, are you?"

He has seen through your bluff. What are you going to do now? There are eight of them and only one of you.

If you think you it would be best to avoid this confrontation by trying to make a dash for it, go to **207**. If you would rather follow up your warning with a show of force by casting a spell at your foes, go to **197**.

202

It's the leader who is responsible for this treatment, and it will pay. You can only hope that getting the leader out of the way will scare the other two into retreating.

Arcane words fall rapidly from your lips as you begin to cast your spell. You feel the magic forces gathering, harnessed by your will.

Turn to **10** and cross-index the spell you choose to cast with the number of this section. Continue the adventure by turning to the section listed where the two columns meet.

203

"Humph!" grunts the mage in disgust. "How you ever got this far is anyone's guess. You seem to have cast the right spells at the right times, but your use of your training and natural abilities was at best shoddy! I did not realize you lacked so much."

He pauses, pondering your fate. Then he continues. "I had intended to propose an exchange to you, one that would be of benefit to both of us. Now I see that that is unwarranted. Since you must nevertheless complete the Test, I grant you instead a full complement of spell components. You will be free to use any spell you know during the final phase of your trial. Go now. You would be well advised to petition whatever gods you serve, for you will need all the help they can provide!"

The great mage waves his hands in an arcane pattern and the room fades, leaving you to your fate. Turn to **120**.

204

The door with the red triangle stands before you. It's rather plain and looks pretty much like any other door leading into any other room.

You reach for the handle and slowly turn it. It feels oddly warm to the touch and gives with a soft click. But try as you might, you can't get the door to swing open. In fact, you can't get it to budge at all!

As you attempt to release the handle, you find that your hand is locked in place! You can't remove it! What's worse, the handle is getting warmer—much warmer! As you struggle to free your hand from the burning handle, you realize that the door itself is beginning to smoke! Tiny tongues of flame lick hungrily through the cracks between the boards.

You're sure now that you've gone to the wrong door, but the realization is no help to you now.

Suddenly the door explodes into flames. The force of the explosion showers burning debris all around you and finally knocks you free of the door handle. But by now, the flames have begun to feed on your robes, and you are enveloped in flame. *How could I be so stupid?* is your last conscious thought.

Turn to **117**.

205

You have no idea how long you have sat here alone on the valley floor. You vaguely remember the sun going down—once? . . . twice?—but that doesn't really matter. Caramon is gone, and you have failed.

Caramon! you wail silently. *How can it have happened? He wasn't supposed to die! He wasn't even supposed to be here!*

Once again your thoughts turn to the events at the forest's edge. Your spells had failed, your mind had failed, and your brother was left to fight on his own. The look of shock on his face fills your mind once more. It was the last you saw of him before the beast's final attack.

The ogredog had proven too much for Caramon to handle alone. The two of you had always fought as a team, and you had always won—frequently against more formidable opponents than this! But without your help, against a creature of such size, he didn't stand a chance. Before your unbelieving eyes, the ogredog had torn the last vestige of life from your brother's prostrate body with one vicious jerk of its massive head.

The beast had then turned to look at you. Its red eyes burning hotly with blood-lust, it threw back its head and screamed a victory howl, blood spewing from its gaping maw. You were helpless to stop it from dragging Caramon's body into the dark recesses of the forest.

You failed Caramon when he needed you most. He died,

and he didn't have to. And now you can't even find his body to give it a decent burial. You continue to sit on the ground in a nearly helpless state. Now you can have nothing more to do with the Test. You are overcome by the injustice of it all, the loss of your brother and what that will mean to your life.

You may well sit here grieving for the rest of your life.

206

You can almost feel the Sleep spell touch the lead dragonman. You watch in tense anticipation as its head bobs and its eyes blink. If all goes as planned, the dragonman will soon drop into a deep sleep.

Instead, the dragonman leader merely shakes its head, rubs its eyes, and looks around. A sinking feeling sweeps over you. The leader must be magic resistant!

The dragonman roars angrily and looks in your direction. By some perverse sixth sense, it seems to know just what has happened. As though following the trail of magic with its eyes, it glares into your hiding place. Pointing its mace, it shouts a command to its subordinates.

They turn and draw their swords. Hurriedly you try to cast another spell before they can get to you. Turn to **167**.

207

The bullies continue to circle around you, taunting you and feinting. The two with clubs swing them dangerously close to your head several times.

Panic fills your heart, and your stomach churns in fear.

Suddenly you think you see an opening in the circle. *If I can just make it as far as the woods . . .* you think. Picking what seems to be the proper moment, you make your break.

"Watch him there!" the leader snaps quickly. "We can't be letting him run off, can we, now?" The circle snaps shut tightly around you. You're trapped!

The first bully laughs at you, a soft, evil sound. Then he looks around slowly at his circle of cronies and says, "Well, let's teach this magician a lesson, eh? Get him, boys!"

The ruffians close in on you like a pack of wolves. As they move in, you draw your dagger, but before you can use it, a club crashes down on your hand, and it falls to the ground. Another heavy blow crashes into your head, and you feel your knees buckle as everything starts to go cloudy.

From somewhere in the fog, you can make out a harsh voice. "Let this be a lesson to you, magician," growls the leader, "don't ever try to best your betters!" A hard kick in your back punctuates his remark, and you feel a bone snap in your ribs. The kick is followed by another and another as blows rain painfully all over your body.

No! you shout silently. *It can't end here! I've only just started!*

In horror, you realize that these ruffians are going to beat you to death. Par-Salian's warning about running away from a challenge comes to mind. You tried to run away, and now you are paying the price—with your life. The despair of failure and fear of death knot your stomach tightly as your last scream of pain is cut short by a club that splits open your skull. Turn to **18**.

208

Something about the poem and the symbols on the doors seems to be connected. Suddenly it dawns on you.

Of course! you think. The voice said your past could be

"pure-white, forgiven." The past must lie through the door with the white triangle! Then red must stand for "blood-red death, ever *present*—the present. That leaves black for the future.

It becomes apparent to you that your benefactor would not have given you these clues if it were not important to face the trials in the proper order. Recalling that he mentioned the past first in the list of trials, you head for the door with the white triangle on it. Turn to **99**.

209

With soot and salt in hand, you finish saying the words of your Comprehend Languages spell. Then, in an effort to get closer to the monster, you fling open the door separating you from the chamber.

As you hoped, the enraged monster swiftly reaches through the door to grab you. As the creature's great claw wraps around your body, you reach out and touch its skin. Immediately the ogre's words come to you clearly. You can understand it!

"I am Ghol-an," it shouts, "an ogre mage of my people. Can you understand me so that we may talk?"

You are quick to reply. "Of course, Ghol-an," you say. "I understand you perfectly. What do you wish to talk about?"

The ogre mage blinks its eyes in dumbfounded amazement. Then it throws its head back and cries, "At last! Another chance to escape. Perhaps you are the one who will free me!" Then the creature sits on the sandy floor of its prison to tell you its tale.

"Long years ago I was placed here by evil mages to serve as a part of their ritual. They said my services would only be needed for a short time, but instead they imprisoned me in this foul place."

"But if you are indeed an ogre mage," you say guardedly, "why don't you use your magic to free yourself?"

Ghol-an stands and bellows in rage, flailing at the golden collar around its neck. "Because they tricked me! They placed powerful magic upon me! They had me chained to yonder stone pillar with this massive steel chain and collar! It is magically unbreakable, even by someone of my size and strength. Not only that, but also none of my spells work anymore. It seems that this chamber counteracts my magic. As you can see, I am hopelessly trapped!"

"Well, my poor friend," you begin, chuckling to yourself, "your imprisonment has lasted far too long. The mages who put you here have treated you disgracefully. I'll set that aright by telling you of your deception. Yonder 'pillar' is nothing more than a mere tree trunk, and not a very thick one at that. As for your chain and collar, they are made of the thinnest, softest gold I've ever seen. One as powerful as you should be able to snap them in pieces almost effortlessly."

Looking crestfallen, Ghol-an drops to the floor again. "The others who came have all said the same thing," he says dejectedly, "but I am nevertheless held prisoner by an immense steel chain!"

Roll one die and add the result to your reasoning skill score. If the total is 7 or more, turn to **220**. If it is 6 or less, go to **34**.

210

The disembodied voice of Par-Salian seems to speak directly to your mind, laden with sorrow.

"Fear, Raistlin? You let fear overwhelm you? Sad to say, it seems we have made a mistake. We thought you were ready to face the trials of the Test. We see now that we were wrong. You have much yet to learn. Go, then! Return to your home. Perhaps at some future time you will be offered the opportunity to become what we thought we saw in you. Do not seek us. If the time is right, we will seek you out once more. For the present, farewell."

With that, the voice ceases, and you hear only the soft whisper of the wind. You look out over the valley floor, stunned. *Can it be all over?* you think. *All over, simply because I was afraid? It cannot be! Yet all is gone—the towers, the forest . . . the Test! I have failed before I even started.*

Your heart sinks to new depths of despair. Not only have you lost the opportunity to become a great magician, but you must also return to your school and face the scorn of your associates yourself. You don't even look up at Caramon as you turn your horse to return to your village. Your thoughts are only on your dark, dismal future. You will have to return to the school, there to wait, to learn, and to hope for another chance to face the Test.

211

Cursing, Caramon continues to struggle with his mount. You grab your horse's reins tightly and manage to stay on its back. Leaping to the ground, you lash its reins to a nearby tree. Your eyes scan the swirling mists for some sign of what frightened the horses. You review in your mind the spells you have prepared for the day. Which of them will you have to use first?

As if summoned by your thoughts, magical forces begin to focus around you, and your body tingles with power at the rich magic flow. Caramon's curses slip from your hearing instantly as, almost at the same instant, the power around you crystallizes and you spot the object of your search.

Add 1 extra experience point to your total and turn to **5**.

Torches in sconces along the walls brightly illuminate the room. Steam rises through two large ten foot circular holes in the floor, making the air warm and steamy. Before you, through the smoky mists, you see an amazing device, which occupies most of the room.

Two large wheels are positioned between the two holes in the floor. Over one of the holes hangs a tremendous black pot, attached to a chain. The chain runs from the pot, over the two wheels, and down through the center of the other hole. Just beyond the two wheels is another tunnel opening.

Much to your surprise, the huge pot is filled to the brim with squirming gully dwarves. Some of them are even hanging onto the sides of the pot. One of them, however, isn't anywhere near the pot.

A female gully dwarf kneels a few feet away from the pot. Obviously in great pain, she has her face upturned, glaring defiantly at her tormentors as they lash her with a long whip.

Standing over her, whip in hand, is a creature the likes of which you have never seen before and hope never to see again. It looks like a part of some twisted and horrible nightmare.

Roll one die and add the result to your presence ability score. If you saw the face of the spectral minion in the Wayreth Forest, subtract 1 point. If the total is 6 or more, turn to **122**. If it is less than 6, or if you have no spells left to cast, turn to **138**.

213

A cloud of inky darkness spreads from the tiny piece of coal you hold in your hand as your Darkness spell takes effect. The cloud swirls and deepens until you are hidden from the ogre by a black void.

Confused, the ogre makes no move toward you but instead stands at the door shouting something you cannot understand.

Since the ogre can't seem to find you, you have time to try another spell by turning to **10**. However, if this was the third spell you have cast and you still don't understand what the ogre is saying, go to **181**.

214

"Well, that's that," he says cheerily. "And all in all, you handled it pretty well, too, I'd say. But then, I'm not one of your judges. I'm just a phantasm, a figment of your imagination. Besides, this part of the Test was easy. What's waiting for you will be a lot harder. If you haven't been there yet, you must now head on up the road to Verdin and continue your trials there. If you've already seen the cleric up there, just wait right here. You can't tell what might happen along."

Before you can speak a word, he fades into the air and disappears, leaving you with many unanswered questions.

If you haven't been to Verdin yet, turn to **7**. If you've already been to Verdin, turn to **131** and wait to see what "happens along."

As the voice stops speaking, you see a faint light that gradually begins to grow coming from somewhere. Quickly you search for its source. When you look down, you see a small circle of light between your feet.

But even as you watch, the circle of light is getting larger. The longer you watch, the bigger it gets. Suddenly you are falling, dropping through the air with ever increasing speed! Now you can see shapes and features within the circle of light below you. You are falling from what must be hundreds of feet above the courtyard of the towers!

Your thoughts race wildly. *Do the Shapers of the Test mean to destroy me at the outset, or is this a part of my trial?*

Again the rasping voice enters your mind. Somehow its dusky whisper calms your turbulent thoughts.

"Now here is entertainment indeed, young mage! I would ask you a question, though. Is all that seems real actually real?"

"Riddles!" you reply hotly. "I'm falling to my death and you ask me riddles?"

"Think," your invisible mentor admonishes. "All I ask is that you think."

Roll one die and add the result to your reasoning skill score. If the total is less than 7, go to **92**. If it is 7 or more, turn to **16**.

216

As the fog parts, the very trees begin to move aside, revealing a narrow path through the underbrush. Someone or something has cleared a way for you to enter!

But more astounding still is the creature that now crashes its way through the misty undergrowth to stand at the edge of the forest. Even in your wildest dreams you could never have imagined such a thing.

It appears to be a horrible cross between a gigantic hairless dog and an ogre, easily as tall as your horses. In its thick, flat head burn two glowing red eyes above a tremendous maw full of fangs. Its great slavering mouth gnashes at the air, as if impatient to chew on anything it contacts. A short, muscular neck connects head to massive body. Great shoulders end in powerfully built front legs that are slightly longer than its thickly muscled hind legs. Each of its legs ends in a wide, four-toed paw, with talons that look as if they could tear through stone. Its hide is the dull gray of stone itself.

Growling and slavering, its body seeming to expand with each breath, the ogredog moves from the edge of the wood and slowly advances a step or two. It looks first at you, then at Caramon, as though trying to decide which of you to tear apart first. Suddenly it stops, its glowing orbs focused straight at you!

Throwing back its great head in a bloodcurdling howl, it prepares to attack.

Roll one die and add the result to your agility skill score. If the total is 7 or more, turn to **100**. If it is less, go to **45**.

Instantly you release your Hold Portal spell on the door, and not a moment too soon. Even as you complete the words, the ogre tries to reach through the door to grab you, but its hand merely thuds against the door and bounces off. It looks at the door quizzically and pushes at it again, but it still doesn't open. It steps back a pace and shouts once more.

You know that your spell won't hold the door for long, but at least you've bought yourself enough time to cast another spell by turning to **10**. However, if this was the third spell you've cast and you still don't know what the ogre mage is trying to tell you, turn to **181**.

218

A tiny piece of spiderweb dangles from the end of your finger. As you recite the words of your Web spell, it floats gently over to where the two smaller dragonmen are standing and lands unseen behind them.

Immediately it starts to grow. Sticky tendrils of web shoot up from the floor. Startled, the dragonmen look down at their feet as the tendrils begin to wrap around their legs, but before they can free themselves, another group of web tendrils spills down from the ceiling. Soon the two dragonmen are completely entangled in the webbing. As they struggle, it enwraps them even more tightly.

The dwarves roar in laughter. The lead dragonman, however, isn't laughing. It clangs the side of the pot with its mace to silence the dwarves. Then it jumps to the side of the pot and grabs hold of the chain. As the pot begins to sink through the hole in the floor, the dragonman pulls a small object from a pouch at its belt. Muttering to itself, it jumps into the pot and disappears from sight.

Make a check of your reasoning skill. Roll one die and add the result to your reasoning skill score. If the total is 8 or more, turn to **146**. If it is less than 8, go to **37**.

219

Dull, throbbing pain is your first indication that you aren't dead—not that you might not actually prefer death to the way you feel now.

Slowly you gather what little strength remains and attempt to open your eyes. Instantly you wish you hadn't. The light that pierces your eyes only serves to sharpen the ache in your head. Quickly you let your eyelids drop shut again.

The sound of wind chimes fills the air around you. Through the tinkling, you can make out a voice.

"So, you have finally rested long enough, have you? Good! Please open your eyes now and sit up. I have a message to deliver to you, and your little nap has already cost me more time than I care to spend."

You struggle again to open your eyes. What you see causes you to sit bolt upright. A quick scan of the room you find yourself in almost takes your breath away. You've seen a mage's workroom before, but you've never seen one so complete with wonderful—and terrible—items for the working of magic. Rows of shelves line the walls, holding countless bottles and vials filled with spell components. As you make a quick survey, you see a large table underneath the shelving, also filled with magical paraphernalia. Everywhere you look you see instruments and devices used in the research of magic. Some of them you don't even begin to recognize.

But even more breathtaking is the creature that stands next you. Turn to **21**.

220

As the ogre mage sits dejectedly on the sandy floor of its prison, an idea suddenly flashes into your head.

"Well, then," you say, "I'll have to show you that what I say is true. Let's do a little test, shall we? Hand me a portion of the chain that binds you.... That's it, just slide some of it through the door. You're in for a great surprise."

Hesitantly, as you speak, the great ogre pushes open the door and slides a small part of the thin chain through the opening. Then the creature's eyes almost start out of its head, for as the chain passes out of the chamber, the magic spell disguising it is broken. You can tell from Ghol-an's expression that the creature finally recognizes the tiny gold chain for what it really is!

The effect is astounding. Immediately Ghol-an jumps to its feet and seizes the chain between its massive hands. With a flick of the wrists and a shout of joy, the ogre mage snaps the chain in two.

Instantly another amazing thing happens. The door simply disappears! You feel a strange flowing sensation sweeping by you as the magic from the tower begins to flow into the ogre mage's prison chamber once more.

Ghol-an senses what has happened. Immediately the huge creature leaps into the air and begins to soar around the cavern. Once, twice, three times the ogre passes by you, laughing like a child at its newly recovered freedom. On its third pass, it comes to a stop in the air before you.

"Young mage, you have set me free," Ghol-an says exultantly. "I am forever in your debt. If our paths ever cross again, your every wish will be my command. For now, though, I will tell you that a great treasure awaits you up yonder tunnel—a treasure of utmost importance to the success of your Test. I wish you luck!"

With that, Ghol-an soars out of the cavern and up the tunnel you entered through, laughing all the while. Turn to **142**.

221

You emerge from your hiding place and race into the tunnel as fast as you can. Those dwarves were making good time, and you don't want to lose them.

After about thirty feet, the tunnel turns sharply to the left. You find yourself in a long hall, with dark alcoves on either side. A yellow-orange light shines dimly from an opening at the far end of the hall. The dwarves stop and huddle before the opening, as though waiting for something. The gong sounds again and they rush toward the light.

In a few moments you, too, are at the opening, but now you hear some disturbing sounds coming from the other room. It sounds like a whip lashing out, followed by cries of pain and fear. Then you hear a strange laugh and commands in a language you have never heard before. Low, guttural noises sound as if they are made by the gully dwarves. These are quickly silenced by the clanging sound of metal on metal. Then the lash falls again, and you hear another cry of pain.

Cautiously you peer out into the light. Turn to **212**.

222

"But before you proceed," Fistandantalus interjects, "I have something else for you."

He passes his hand in the air before him. The air shimmers and congeals, and as it solidifies, it becomes . . .

"A staff!" you exclaim.

"Yes," says Fistandantalus, "the Staff of Magius! I kept it back from you earlier, hoping you would prove your prowess in battle. You have now convinced me by your courage, pluck, and magical skill that you are worthy of your opponent. It contains a Continual Light spell you'll need to defeat the drow—and much, much more, as you will see!"

You gaze in awe at the staff. One end is covered with bright metal, and at the other end, you see a claw holding a small glass ball. As you reach for the staff, it quivers and leaps into your hand of its own volition! As soon as you grab it, you know it—what it does, its spells how it can serve and protect you.

With renewed confidence, you turn to face the drow for the final time. Turn to **194**.

223

You know now what you must do—try to cast a Detect Invisibility spell and find the dragonman! You turn and kneel casually beside the gully dwarf, bending over her to hide your movement. Swiftly you reach inside your robe and remove the components for your spell. Mumbling softly, you sprinkle the talc and powdered silver in front of you.

Out of the corner of your eye, you see the dragonman! Trying to get behind you, the lead dragonman is skulking along the wall to your right! If it had succeeded in avoiding detection, Gilean only knows what would have happened, but it hasn't succeeded—not yet!

You begin to recite the words of your spell. This one will have to do the dragonman in or you'll be at his mercy!

But the dragonman seems to sense what you intend. It snarls loudly and prepares to attack.

Roll one die and add the result to your agility skill score. If the total is 7 or more, turn to **60**. If it is 6 or less, or if you have no spells left to cast, turn to **153**.

224

Safely hidden in the dark niche, you watch to see what comes out of the opening.

Into the dim light of the great hall charges a small army of short, strange beings. There seem to be about twenty of the filthy little creatures. Their size and unkempt appearance instantly make you think of the gully dwarves that your friend, Flint Fireforge, cursed so often. How these filthy creatures could have caused him any trouble is beyond you.

The gully dwarves in the lead skid to a halt as soon as they enter the large room. The rest crash into the ones in the front, and they all end up in an untidy pile of dirty arms and legs. They manage to untangle themselves and stare about dumbly, as if they're unable to remember where they are or what they are doing here. An argument breaks out in the group, but before it goes too far, the gong sounds once more. The creatures leap up in fear, then form in a tight huddle. In seconds, they break from the huddle and speed off down the tunnel.

Gully dwarves? you think. *What are gully dwarves doing here? And what, if anything, do they have to do with my Test?*

On further thought, however, you realize that you could always retrace your steps back to this room, and you decide to follow the gully dwarves. Turn to **221**.

225

How you could ever have been so stupid is a question you may never get a chance to answer. You stare numbly at the now inert body of the dead gully dwarf. Your spell was of no consequence at all. It didn't serve to stop the beating, and now she is dead.

Not only that, but your inept magic use has given your hiding place away! The lead dragonman is shouting orders at his underlings. They turn and begin to advance toward you. Turn to **167**.

226

You look up, blood drooling from your mouth, to see Fistandantalus standing before you. His hood has been thrown back from his head, revealing a strong, youthful face!

"I have completed our bargain," shouts Fistandantalus. "A part of your life for success!"

"But—but I am dying," you croak, coughing again. "Surely this cannot be all of life you will leave me. The

184

pain is too great to bear!"

"Do not be concerned, Raistlin," says the mage, glorying in his newfound strength. "You will learn to live with the pain, and there are medicines you will find to ease your discomfort. Think instead of the rewards of coexistence with me. The pain should seem little enough in view of that. And who knows what the future will bring?"

He laughs deeply. "Now I must go. The matter of a battle requires my immediate attention. But be warned that this transformation will have a marked effect on the way you see life from now on. I have worked a subtle but powerful magic upon you, so that your eyes, your very sight, have been changed. Death will be ever before you, your constant companion. All that you see will be consumed in your eyes by the slow process of dying, reminding you always of your frailty and mortality. Let that, along with the staff, serve to recall to your mind our bargain."

He pauses to chuckle. "How foolish of me to say that," he says thoughtfully. "When I depart, all memory of our exchange will pass from your mind, but then—you will remember!"

He turns to leave. "Farewell again, mage! You have triumphed, though at great cost. Your brother has been sent to help you back to the towers, for there is much yet for you to learn. But you can rest assured that Par-Salian will see to that. And you live long enough to do so!"

As Caramon appears in the cavern, Fistandantalus fades from view. But the mage's last words echo softly in your mind. "Go now, Raistlin! One day your strength will save the world!"

EPILOGUE

Caramon did come and carry the wounded, dying Raistlin to the safety of the towers. And there Raistlin received what healing was possible. The twins eventually left the Towers of High Sorcery, but there was a different feeling between them.

For true to the foreshadowing of Fistandantalus, though Raistlin never did remember his encounter with the great mage, Par-Salian was not finished with the young mage yet. There was one last test, though not a part of *the* Test, that both Raistlin and his brother would have to face together. It would change their relationship forever.

But that is not chronicled here. "The Test of the Twins" can only be found recounted in one of the obscure annals of Astinus of Palanthus (*Dragon* Magazine #83) or in the Chronicles of the Dragonlance. That test binds the twins Raistlin and Caramon irrevocably together, assuring that their fates and the fate of the world of Krynn hang on the same balance.

Advanced Dungeons & Dragons®

ADVENTURE GAMEBOOKS

From the Producers of the DUNGEONS & DRAGONS® Game

- Reads like a book, plays like a game
- YOU determine your character's skills
- Game employs hit points, saving throws, combat, skill points, more

#1 PRISONERS OF PAX THARKAS

#2 THE GHOST TOWER

#3 ESCAPE FROM CASTLE QUARRAS

#4 THE SOULFORGE

TSR, Inc.
PRODUCTS OF YOUR IMAGINATION™

ONE-ON-ONE™ ADVENTURE GAMEBOOKS

by James M. Ward

The ONE-ON-ONE Gamebooks are self-contained role-playing games for two people. Each player becomes the central character in one of the two books. Each book portrays the adventure, step by step, as the two characters stalk each other through a dangerous environment until they reach the final combat!

Play anytime!

Play anywhere!

Play many times!

CASTLE ARCANIA
You are the gallant knight or the powerful wizard, each searching for other in the magical ruins of Castle Arcania.

BATTLE FOR THE ANCIENT ROBOT
You are the human star pilot or the killer robot, racing through space in a desperate search for the powerful parts of the Ancient Robot.

REVENGE OF THE RED DRAGON
You are the vengeful red dragon or the marauding black knight who raided the dragon's lair.

Boxed set of two books includes everything needed to play. All you provide is paper, two pencils, and one friend.

Suggested retail price: $5.95. Available at fine book and hobby stores.

AMAZING™ STORIES:

60 Years of the Best Science Fiction

Edited by Isaac Asimov and Martin H. Greenberg

This anthology features some of the best stories from the early days of America's first and longest-running science-fiction magazine, **AMAZING®
Science Fiction Stories**. This trade paperback book is enhanced by full-color reproductions of sixteen covers photographed from the original magazines.

The anthology includes stories published as early as 1928. Some of the authors represented are Isaac Asimov, Ursula K. Le Guin, John Jakes, Philip José Farmer, Robert Bloch, and Philip K. Dick.

240 pages • $7.95   **JUNE 1985**

Distributed to the book trade in the U.S. by Random House, Inc., and in Canada by Random House of Canada, Ltd.